Class Encounters

Class Encounters

by

Mark H. Meuser

RIVERCROSS PUBLISHING, INC.
Orlando

Printed in the United States of America. No part of this book may be used or reproduced in any manner whatsoever without written permission, except in the case of brief quotations embodied in critical articles and reviews. For information address RIVERCROSS PUBLISHING, INC., 127 East 59th Street, New York, NY 10022 or editor@rivercross.com.

ISBN: 1-58141-015-8

Library of Congress Catalog Card Number: 99-055107

Library of Congress Cataloging-in-Publication Data

Meuser, Mark H., 1949-
    Class encounters/by Mark H. Meuser.
      p. cm.
    ISBN 1-58141-015-8
    1. Teacher-student relationships—United States—Fiction. 2. High school teachers—United Sates—Fiction 3. Education, Secondary—United States—Fiction 4. High schools—United States—Fiction I. Title.

PS3563.E74644 C57 1999
813'.54—dc21   99-055107

To my wife Susan and daughter Anne

Acknowledgments

I am indebted to many people for the publication of this book. To all of them I express my sincere thanks.

Mark A. Miller, a colleague and good friend, was untiring in his encouragement, invaluable in his editing, and unfailing in his insistence that I write in active voice. It was Mark who convinced me that I could write the book, and for that I will always be grateful. David J. Hogan, author, editor, and friend, reviewed the manuscript and offered much-appreciated expertise. Josh Furman, editor at Rivercross, generously provided the professional help and encouragement needed to transform the manuscript into a book.

Many friends, colleagues, and relatives read and proofread the manuscript. Kim Bainter, Jim Birath, Carole Bickel, Rod Calloway, Connie Corey, Marilyn Hedrick, Donna Langhals, Joe and Kathy Mailander, John and Susan Meuser, Alan and Linda Mittermaier, Mary Lou Purdy, Joann Roszman, Sue Schneider, Robert and Janet Southgate, Lorraine Stuckey, Janet Thomas, Linda Weinstock, and Michele Winship read all or selected parts of the manuscript, offering valuable advice. Randy Allen provided the technological assistance to ready the manuscript for submission. All of my recent classes at school served as test audiences for several of the stories. Their reactions helped me edit and revise many of them. I am grateful to my father, L. H. Meuser, for always expressing enjoyment at what I write.

I would especially like to thank my wife Susan and daughter Anne for their continued patience and support during the seemingly endless process of writing and publishing a book.

Contents

Foreword

I began to know Mark Meuser long before I met him, even though we taught on the same faculty. In 1985, still in my 20s, I started teaching English at "Bridgeport" High School. Our faculty numbered almost 100 and was divided among three campus buildings filled with nearly 1,500 students. Thus, it was not unusual never to know many of one's colleagues. I certainly did not know Mark . . . until students, especially seniors, began talking about him in my classes.

In bemused voices, they offered fascinating details about this 30-ish man who taught them mathematics. Neatness, cleanliness, and orderliness remained essential in his classroom. Mark demanded that students use the corners of floor tiles to line up the legs of their desks exactly. Students were responsible for picking up any paper in the territory around them, whether they dropped it there or not. These were givens, and if students did not automatically adhere to these conditions, they faced punishment, usually detention.

Laughing cautiously, students also confided in me that Mark wore a similar outfit nearly every day: dark slacks, sports jacket, white shirt, and tie with a bright gold tie tack. His hair looked perfect, coaxed into place with a substance that gleamed under florescent light.

Students loved him. I decided he was severely, perhaps incurably, anal retentive.

The first time I saw Mark in the presence of students was in a study hall, winter of 1986. A noisy cafeteria full of students became suddenly silent when Mark entered. This was out of respect for his reputation, although at the time I thought it might be from the shock of seeing someone who looked as though he had just swallowed a large ramrod whole. His back perfectly straight, chin up, the air of a practiced epicure all about him, he seemed like royalty.

That spring I stopped by Burger King early one morning before school, on a work day for teachers, sans students. Accordingly, I felt relaxed and dressed that way—shorts and tee-shirt. After I bought my breakfast sandwich, I sauntered toward the dining area. Sitting by himself, in his customary formal outfit, including the tie, was Mark. We made some awkward eye contact, and he nodded his head in a way that suggested that I join him—or *must* join him. Curious, I plopped down in front of him. "Mark Miller," I said, extending a hand of welcome. "Mark Meuser, math teacher," was his reply, with a firm but suspiciously short shake.

It didn't take long to launch into what was turning his neck red. Too many field trips. Students belong in the classroom where *real* learning takes place. A trip one of my fellow English teachers had planned to a Shakespearean production at a nearby university struck him as particularly "ridiculous." *Gee* I thought, *this guy needs someone to mess up his hair a little bit. Doesn't he know that we also read and study Shakespeare in the classroom, so that students will be ready to benefit from the complete experience of an actual performance? I'll tell him.*

Poppycock! came his reply. *You can read the plays in the classroom. That is more than adequate if you are doing your jobs.* Mark and I rolled out of the restaurant's parking lot less than buddies.

When Mark left for a year in England as a part of a teacher exchange program, I was not particularly saddened, and as an Anglophile, I was even looking forward to meeting his replacement from that country.

The year passed quickly, though. Mark was soon back, and students in my British Literature class began repeating his stories about his experiences over there. They were—dare I say it?—*funny*. I decided to forget about the Burger King tirade and invited him to speak in my class. He accepted (I guess *he* felt fine about his Burger King tirade) and seemed excited.

On the appointed day, Mark walked in, rolling a cart with a slide projector on it. I had visions of my own high school days when a history teacher showed us slides from his vacation to Williamsburg. By the end of that presentation, my eyes looked like those of a dead fish, floating on its side in polluted water.

With Mark, it was different. I learned why students loved this teacher I had believed to be narrow-minded. His comments about the slides were so dryly clever and witty that I found myself believing that J. B. Priestley must be speaking, certainly not Mark. We burst into laughter repeatedly, about tasks as ordinary as taking attendance, precisely because Mark brandished a polished technique of making the commonplace seem hilarious. Humor is everywhere, including in the household plumbing, as Mark sees the world. Even better, no one suffers as the victim of Mark's merriment. His humor is affectionate and warm and sprinkled with crushing insight.

I encouraged Mark to write this book after enjoying his visit (and later many others) to my classroom. My only fear was that his humor would not come off so effectively without the live, physical delivery, so well-timed and executed. Part of Mark's secret is that conservative, straight-laced visage of his, which produces a type of comedy not unlike the Queen passing wind. Fortunately, his writing style mirrors that visage perfectly.

Mark's book is also a chronicle of a teacher's growth, or of climbing a mountain, as his simple but eloquent metaphor will reveal. He is one of the best in our profession, and his observations and criticisms are sharp and uncompromising, just as his love and care for his students and the integrity of his position are genuine and heartfelt. Furthermore, I believe that today he would see the value of a field trip to a Shakespearean play, especially after writing this book, for Mark understands the value of reflecting on one's life experiences. You will find the results of these reflections equally rewarding.

Mark A. Miller
25 June 1999

Class Encounters

Introduction
A Glimpse of the Mountain

"I thought I was special," said the speaker. "I was an educator. I had been an outstanding student in college: a Phi Beta
Kappa. I had so much to offer. I knew all the latest methods
of instruction. I knew how to make each one of my students
a success. I thought kids would beat a path to my door.
They didn't."

I sat listening to the keynote speaker at my first-ever re-
gional teachers' conference. I had driven there with my former
college advisor, Dr. Arthur Schiller, and two other math teachers. We had been through two days of meetings and presentations, and I was beyond the saturation point. I had actually
thought of leaving early but never dared to mention such her-
esy to Dr. Schiller.

The conference odyssey had begun uneventfully two days
earliler as I drove to Dr. Schiller's house. It was late March,
and the fresh smell of an early spring rain still hung in the air.
Bits of blue were peeking out from behind patchy gray skies,
a warm breeze was blowing in from the west, and I was
chomping at the bit to get on the open road. The site of the
conference was the modest burg of Middletown. Not exactly

17

New York or Las Vegas, but it held the allure of the unknown. I had been looking forward to it for weeks.

Dr. Schiller lived in an older, yet affluent section of town. I parked in front of his house, took my small suitcase from the trunk, and walked up several steps to his old-fashioned front porch. Wicker furniture was tastefully arranged in a couple of conversation groups. Several potted plants softened the brickwork of the porch. A pile of precisely cut firewood rested in an iron holder expressly made for that purpose. The Schiller porch was a time capsule from the last century. I stood for a while admiring its order.

The front door opened even before I rang the bell. It was Mrs. Schiller. They had been expecting me. She invited me inside, and I was greeted by the most wonderful smell imaginable. It was a complex smell, a combination of freshly baked cookies and wood polish, with a slight hint of pipe tobacco. The interior itself was a plush continuation of the front porch, with comfortable, overstuffed furniture, soft carpets and draperies, and gleaming darkly-stained woodwork. The only visible concession to the twentieth century was a standard black telephone on a small side table at the base of the staircase to the second floor.

Seated on the edge of one of the overstuffed chairs was Bill Burrows, a high school teacher about my age. He looked ill at ease. Mrs. Schiller introduced us and offered me a seat on the couch. She then asked if we would like some cookies. We readily accepted, not only because their smell was irresistible, but also because it would give us something to do while we waited for Dr. Schiller. Bill and I praised the cookies profusely and then settled into an embarrassed silence while prim Mrs. Schiller tried to start conversations about topics that were of little interest to two men at least thirty years her junior.

Finally Dr. Schiller appeared. Bill and I rose to greet him, and he came over to shake our hands.

Dr. Schiller was close to sixty but still cut an impressive figure. Although his hair was gray and thinning, his demeanor was robust and his handshake firm. His thin gray mustache and tanned face gave him the look of an English country squire. Actually, this wasn't too far off the mark, as he had a tree farm south of the city that he ran in his spare time.

"Sorry I am running a little late," he said. "My last class ran a little past. Anyway, are we all ready to go?"

We told him we were ready. We said our good-byes to Mrs. Schiller and took our suitcases to the curb while Dr. Schiller went to fetch the car. It was in the garage off the alley behind his house, and he had to drive it around to the front so we could load up. Bill and I waited by the curb for what seemed to be quite some time. Eventually, we noticed an ancient Rambler rounding the corner and heading very slowly for us. We looked at each other and then at the car again, realizing almost instantly, even from a block away, that its driver was Dr. Schiller. In those days, not many men still wore an old-style fedora, the type that he preferred. This driver wore one tilted at a jaunty angle.

The Rambler was in pristine condition, highly waxed and without a trace of the usual car junk inside. The unmistakable odor of pipe tobacco permeated the interior, but it was not altogether unpleasant. It was a two-door model. Bill took the initiative and climbed into the back seat. That left me to sit up front with Dr. Schiller. Although I respected and liked him well enough, I didn't know if I could keep up a conversation with him for the entire two-hour trip. I needn't have worried.

"We have to pick up a friend of mine," said Dr. Schiller. "His name is Dr. Milford, and he lives over by the university. He's a professor emeritus there now. I'm sure we'll have a lot to talk about."

We drove there slowly through back streets that were unfamiliar to either Bill or me. After picking up his friend, Dr. Schiller cautiously and with noticeable reluctance entered the ramp to the freeway which would take us to Middletown.

The time on the road passed quickly, even though Dr. Schiller drove five to ten miles per hour slower than most of the rest of the traffic. We were ensconced in the right lane of the freeway, and cars whizzed past us on our left. On those rare occasions when we actually passed a car, Bill would look over at me and jerk his head back as though Dr. Schiller had

19

gunned the engine and the car had actually sped up. I would have to stifle a laugh.

As Dr. Schiller had promised, the conversation never flagged. To be honest, I was at first a little intimidated by Dr. Milford. He was a nationally known educator, and I was a second-year teacher. Yet he never used this obvious difference to subjugate my opinions to his. He did have strong opinions about teaching in general and about teaching math in particular. He was one of the educators responsible for the now-infamous "new math." I disagreed with much of what he said and secretly thought that he had been out of a real classroom too long. He was a truly humble man, though, and he argued points of pedagogy with Bill and me as though he were talking with colleagues of equal stature.

We finally arrived at the conference, checked into our hotel rooms, and decided we could make a couple of sessions before dinner. The presentations were informative, but I think I was too tired and hungry to get much out of them. Dinner that evening was a banquet served by the conference organizers. Drs. Schiller and Milford were seized upon by some old friends. Bill and I insisted that they go with their friends. We then found two empty seats at a table with several ladies, one of whom was just one year from retirement.

"You gotta watch these kids nowadays," she said. "They'll cheat if you give 'em half a chance."

Such an abrasive conversational opening startled me a bit. I took a closer look at its source. She was somewhere around sixty with short, but untidy gray hair. She wore no make-up, and the lines in her face had been etched into a permanent scowl. She reminded me of a couple of teachers I had had in school.

"Not all kids are dishonest," I ventured.

"How long you been teachin'?" she snapped. Her words were a verbal epee. She waited for my response only so she could properly finish me off.

"Not that long," I said, not wanting to admit that I was only in my second year.

"Well, I've been at it for thirty years, and I've seen all their tricks. Nuthin' surprises me anymore. You wait till you've been at it a while. Then tell me how far you trust any of 'em."

20

I didn't say anything, and the conversation drifted to other matters. As it turned out, "Mrs. Sourpuss" had some great ideas for teaching a wide range of topics. She was also one of the conference organizers and had been instrumental in getting local businesses to contribute free information for the packets that each teacher received. I didn't doubt that she could wrangle just about anything out of an unsuspecting businessman! She was probably a good teacher if you could get past her sullen disposition. But I vowed then that if I ever became that jaded, I would get out of teaching altogether.

The two-and-a-half day conference was a great success. I had been told that if I came away with one good idea then it was worthwhile. I had several pages of notes with so many wonderful ideas that I wanted to try out in my classes at home. I was excited yet at the same time, exhausted.

The conference organizers had decided to schedule their premier speaker as the last presentation of the last day of the conference. Normally, this would result in a poorly attended final session. In this instance, though, that was anything but the case. The speaker was Birdie Langley, and there was not an empty seat in the auditorium. Veteran conference-goers knowingly assured me that I was in for a treat as we waited for Miss Langley to be introduced.

After a brief, but glowing introduction, Birdie Langley walked onto the stage. She was somewhere in the neighborhood of fifty years old, tall with iron gray hair. She had on a nice suit which seemed slightly ill-fitting. As she approached the podium, she appeared to lean forward as though she were walking into a strong wind. She looked awkward, to say the least. I remember thinking that, because I was near the back, I could sneak out if she wasn't very good.

Then she started to speak, and all thoughts of leaving evaporated into thin air. She talked so fast that I had to strain to hear every word. She reminded me of Groucho Marx. In fact, a couple of times I almost thought I saw a cigar in her hand as she paced back and forth across the stage.

She warmed up the audience with a few humorous stories and soon had us completely in the palm of her hand. She drew from a vast reservoir of experience to relate stories of

21

teaching strategies that worked and those that didn't. She eventually told us about her first teaching assignment and the frustration she had experienced.

"Yes, I was a Phi Beta Kappa, but I couldn't figure out why no one was coming to me for help. I had made myself available before and after school for tutoring, and yet, no one was coming. My students didn't seem to really respect or trust me. Didn't they know how smart I was and how much I could teach them?

"There were only two teachers in that school who were really respected: the football coach and the choir director. Now I could understand why the football coach was respected. He was the only coach in the school, and most of the boys played on the team. But the choir director, now, that was a puzzle.

"It wasn't until I was chaperoning the backstage area during a choir concert that I found out why the choir director was not just respected, but actually loved. Taking a small break from my duties backstage, I walked to the edge of the stage, just behind the curtain where no one in the audience could see me. I could see most of the choir members' faces. I could also see the director's face. I decided to watch for a while.

"They were performing an arrangement of 'America the Beautiful.' Fifty pairs of eyes were on the director's. The singers were intensely focused. As they neared the climax, the director's arm shot into the air, and his eyes opened wide and glistened with anticipation. At that precise moment the bass section exploded with the opening lines of the final verse of the hymn. A similar gesture followed, and the sopranos soared above the rest of the choir with a spine-tingling descant. A small tear formed in the lower corner of my right eye. I had come under their spell. As the piece concluded, the entire choir sang as with one voice, moved as with one body, and spoke to all who would listen as with one soul. It was magnificent.

"The audience was on its feet almost before the last note was over. But the director's first looks were into the eyes of his choir members. He smiled briefly but proudly and mouthed the words 'well done' before turning to the audience to acknowledge their applause. I knew then why he was loved by his students.

"And I knew why I wasn't. He touched the strings of their hearts, while I had managed only to toot my own horn. From that moment on, I had a new goal in teaching. I wanted to touch my students' hearts just like that choir director. The only problem was that I didn't have a clue as to how to do it.

"In the years since that catharsis, I have discovered the clue. It is simple, yet difficult. You have to care about your students. And you have to let your students know that you care about them without actually telling them that you do.

"Many of you, I'm sure, have known this for a long time. Others may still be searching for the clue. To all of you I wish the best in touching the strings of your students' hearts. If you're lucky, you'll find that they will touch the strings of your own heart, too! Thank you very much."

Like the choir of her story, she had us in her spell. We rose to our feet and applauded her enthusiastically. I wanted to talk with her afterward, but the crowd around her after she finished was large, and my colleagues were anxious to start the trip home. I reluctantly left the auditorium.

I didn't talk much during the trip home. I was lost in thought. All the notes that I had taken on teaching techniques seemed to lose importance when compared with the closing words of Birdie Langley's speech. I wanted to be a teacher like her, one who would touch students' hearts. And even though she had told us, I really didn't have a clue how to do that.

At the conference, I had met teachers who were preoccupied with pedagogy and those who were bitter over having spent thirty years with people they didn't like. I didn't want to be either.

"You're all awfully quiet," said Dr. Schiller to the rest of us as we motored along the freeway. The only other noise discernible above the hum of the engine was the sound of cars speeding past us on our left.

"I can't stop thinking about Birdie Langley's talk," I confessed.

"Yeah, she's really something," he responded. "Most teachers never really get to her level of teaching. You know, you've got to trudge through the foothills before you can ascend the mountain. It just takes time."

Leave it to wise old Dr. S. to come up with an apt analogy. I wondered then whether I would ever reach the mountain. In the years that followed, I often thought I caught a glimpse of that mountain. Sometimes I thought I was even ascending it. But the mountain is covered in mist, and the only way to tell whether you're on it is for others to see you there.

Year after year, I trek through the foothills in search of the mountain. Every autumn a different group of students joins me. With each new class and each fresh face, the perennial journey begins anew.

I. Teaching: It's Harder Than It Looks
First Steps

My own journey through the educational foothills had begun in the middle of the previous school year. But the terrain was really more swampland than foothills, with large patches of quicksand at irregular intervals.

Because I had decided late in my junior year of college to become a teacher, I had to complete my student teaching after I graduated in June. After completing that requirement in early December, I began the search for a position. Mid-year jobs were somewhat scarce. Luckily, I managed to find and interview for two jobs that had opened up. One was in the affluent city of Essex, the other in Bridgeport.

I really wanted the Essex job. That school was a palace. The opening was for classes of second-year algebra and geometry, not the typical low-level mathematics that beginning teachers usually get stuck with. Essex had a wide-ranging and well-respected academic curriculum, a first-rate fine arts department, a flourishing industrial arts program, and varied athletic extra-curriculars, including swimming, which I had done in college. Their natatorium put most college pools to shame.

Bridgeport was my second choice. It was a smaller school than Essex. It served a town that was in the midst of changing from a little farming community to a sought-after suburb of a large metropolitan area. The high school building itself was less than ten years old and had a definite "sixties" look to it. Upon entering, I was first struck by its unfinished appearance. Unsightly wiring and gas lines were suspended just below the ceilings of the hallways (a cost-saving measure, I later found out). The interior walls were a mishmash of plasterboard and cement block, painted a nondescript neutral that didn't quite cover in all places. Nevertheless, the place was neat and tidy, and the classrooms were roomy and light, with floor-to-ceiling windows forming the exterior wall of each.

My Bridgeport interview had evidently gone well. Two days afterward, I received a job offer. I waited one more day to find out about the Essex job. Hearing nothing, I decided to accept the Bridgeport "bird in hand." It was fortunate that I did. I soon learned that the Essex job went to a candidate who had done his student teaching there. I probably never really had a chance at it.

At least I had a job. My teaching assignment was five classes of Algebra I, the lowest math class offered at Bridgeport. I was replacing a teacher whom the students had driven from the classroom. No one actually said this in so many words. The principal said euphemistically that he and his students had "reached an impasse." Fellow teachers maintained that the administration had purposefully given him five horrible classes in an effort to drive him out of teaching. Whatever the case, those classes were hardly designed to nurture a first-year teacher. They served more as a baptism by fire.

As I approached my first day, I felt competent in my knowledge of mathematics. I knew I had received excellent training in classroom theory and procedures. My student teaching had gone very well. I should have been brimming with confidence. I was terrified.

For those unfamiliar with teaching, I should point out that every classroom full of students has a group personality. That personality is actually more than the sum total of its individual members. Classes can be funny, caring, rude, or hostile. A

26

teacher can direct and shape a class's personality. However, when a class has been established for three months, it is difficult, if not impossible, to do much "shaping."

"My name is Mr. Meuser," I began in my first period class. Perhaps they sensed the inexperience in my voice.

"Are we going to have homework every day?" someone yelled.

"We will have homework most nights, but I'll try to give you some class time to work on it," I said. I took the question at its face value and not as the challenge to my authority that it probably was. I was going to continue with my class rules, but I evidently paused too long between sentences.

"Mr. Blanchard was a terrible teacher," a girl in the back row loudly blurted out. "You know he was fired. I hope you're better than he was."

"I liked Mr. Blanchard," said another student. "If you guys had been nicer to him, he wouldn't have left."

This prompted loud, simultaneous responses from most of the other students in the room, each stating his opinion of Mr. Blanchard or of the student's comment. It was less than two minutes into the period, and the room had disintegrated into chaos. My initial terror turned to panic. I had to try to regain control.

"Quiet," I yelled. There was some subsiding of the noise level. "I said, 'Quiet.'" This time the talking stopped.

"I can see why Mr. Blanchard quit!" I stated emphatically. There was silence. "I was about to tell you what my classroom rules are."

"Oh, no, another Hitler," said a boy named Martin.

Instead of going after Martin, as I should have done, I attempted to defend my rules, which were as yet unknown to the class.

"I don't have many rules," I said. "You must be in your seats when the bell rings, and you may not talk out of turn. You must keep a folder for your homework and tests. Now let's get started on some algebra and see what you know."

After some grumbling, they all produced paper and pencil and began working on problems that I put on the board. We discussed the solutions, and I thought they were understanding some of the concepts behind those solutions. At this stage of my mathematical development, I frankly did not totally understand everything I was teaching. I could do the problems, but the "correct" solutions were "my" solutions because I didn't know enough to recognize legitimate alternatives. Even with such a dogmatic approach, I did emphasize understanding the process over getting the right answer. My pedagogical training had not been entirely wasted.

The class concluded without further incident. They were certainly not quiet, and not all of them were listening to me all of the time. At least they weren't all yelling at once. Someone in the hallway passing by my class could, I thought, mistake it for one which had a real teacher and where real learning was taking place.

I was physically drained. I was mentally exhausted. I was sweating. It was 8:50 AM. I had barely begun the day.

Periods two and three went a little better. There were no loud outbursts. Even so, I felt that I was talking to about half of them, with the other half talking to each other. They were not like the students I had grown up with. The classes I had been in as a high school student just four years earlier had been well behaved. No one would dare speak out of turn, let alone interrupt a teacher. I didn't understand how these students could be so different.

Mercifully, I had a preparation period next. The math and science departments shared a small office. I walked in and collapsed onto the seat next to my assigned drawer. Carol Foster and Shirley Horne, both science teachers, were there quietly talking. They both seemed so relaxed and at-home. Didn't they have these same kids to teach? Weren't they nervous wrecks just thinking about having to face them in less than an hour? Although I thought these questions, I certainly didn't ask them out loud.

"How's it going?" asked Carol.

"Fine," I said automatically.

"Those classes gave Mr. Blanchard fits," she said. "I'm surprised they haven't revolted on you."

"Well, to be honest, they do talk a lot. I don't think I got very much accomplished. How do you deal with students who never stop talking?"

"I just threaten them with an extra-hard lab. That usually does the trick."

"You know, Mark," interjected Shirley, "I have an advantage over a lot of teachers when it comes to student discipline. I really don't care whether students like me. But I insist that they respect me."

I found out later that students really did respect Shirley. Her comment, though, was a summary of her philosophy of the student-teacher relationship. What I wanted then were a few practical suggestions on how to keep thirty kids quiet while I tried to teach them the quadratic formula.

It was soon time for my fifth period class. Believe it or not, my morning classes had been educational oases compared to fifth period. When my back was turned in that class, they threw spit wads at the board and placed a tack on my chair. Even worse than that was the presence of a girl named Leslie. Leslie was a compulsive talker. Talking was like breathing to her. Asking her not to talk was like asking her not to breathe. She would talk to anybody, including herself. She talked the entire period. I think she had developed the ability to talk even while breathing in. Of course she knew virtually no mathematics. How could she learn anything when she never stopped talking long enough to listen? Leslie made a bad class unbearable. It was at this point that I truly envied Mr. Blanchard. After all, he was not here and I was.

Somehow I made it through the period. Never was I so appreciative of a lunch break. I walked to the cafeteria.

"Are you a teacher?" asked the woman behind the cafeteria cash register.

"Yes," I said. I was twenty-two years old, although I think I looked about seventeen. I had worn a jacket and tie, hoping to look the part of a teacher. If this woman couldn't tell I was a teacher, though, was it any wonder that my students were not treating me as one?

"This is my first day on the job," I volunteered. "I'm taking Mr. Blanchard's place."

"Oh. I'm sorry I had to ask, honey. You just look so young," she said.

A comment that I would revel in now literally cut me to the quick then. I slunk into a seat at the faculty table.

Dining there was not all I had expected it to be either. The teachers at the high school of my student days had a glass-enclosed room in which to lunch. It must have been quiet and relaxing in there. Of course, no students were ever permitted inside. The faculty table at which I was now seated was in the middle of the students' dining area. It offered no privacy and plenty of noise. I didn't have to shout to be heard by others at the table, but almost. Lunch was certainly not relaxing. Afterward, my stomach seemed to be paying the price for a hastily gobbled meal.

Sixth period followed lunch. It wasn't a bad class. The students must have been ready for a nap after eating. Although most of them were not paying attention, at least they weren't talking. I was thankful for small favors.

During seventh period, I shared a study hall duty with another teacher. It was bliss compared with teaching. The end of the day couldn't have come soon enough. I was tired and extremely frustrated, and I had the uncomfortable feeling that my deodorant was not working all that well.

As I drove home after school, I thought, "What have you done to yourself?"

It had to get better than this.

Don't Get Even, Get Mad

Actually, things didn't seem to get any better, at least not for a while.

The problem was that few of my students felt compelled to do what I asked them. They didn't do their homework, they didn't listen in class, and they talked to each other while I was trying to teach. The situation was almost intolerable. My student teaching had not really prepared me for this. My cooperating teacher had always been nearby if not in the room. That threat alone had been enough to keep the kids in line. Now, in my own classroom, I was the final threat, and that was no threat at all.

I tried to fight back with strict rules about no talking. Talking out of turn meant doing an extra assignment. I handed these out quite frequently, and eventually the room became noticeably quieter. I was able to teach a lesson without being interrupted, but the classroom took on the air of a boot camp. There had to be a better way than this. I knew there were teachers who could relax with their classes and yet were able to maintain control. One of these teachers was Old Tom Kennebrew. I decided to talk with him and find out his secret.

Old Tom was about fifty, but he looked sixty-five. Maybe this was why his name was never spoken without the adjective *old* preceding it. His gray hair was slicked down and combed straight back, and his face had a reddish hue, probably from his habit of consuming a six-pack of beer every evening. He looked like he could have stepped right out of a Depression-era gangster movie. Old Tom had taught social studies at almost every secondary building in the district. He was the bane of each of his administrator's existence and had been shuffled around the district like a hot potato. He was a good, if unconventional, teacher and, fortunately for him, had earned tenure in the district many years ago. He had the habit of saying whatever popped into his head to any student, teacher, or administrator who happened to be nearby. His comments were usually witty but sometimes crude. Being a student of history, he had great insight into the politics of any human situation, and what he said usually hit the mark. It was no wonder that administrators were not fond of him.

"How do you keep control of your classes and still have such a relaxed atmosphere in the room?" I asked Old Tom one day in the science office.

"I'll tell you what I do," said Old Tom, moving his hand down his pliable, leathery face and letting out a tired sigh. "Every now and then I plan a good mad."

"A what?" I asked.

"A mad. I pretend to be boiling mad at somebody. When a class thinks they know me a little too well, I just decide to blow my top at the first little provocation. Works like a charm."

"I'm not sure I can do that," I confessed.

"You don't actually have to get mad," said Old Tom. "Just pretend to be mad. It works just as well. The kids don't know the difference."

"I just don't know," I said.

"What have you got to lose?" he countered.

"Good point," I said. "I'll try it."

I decided to attempt it during my first period class the next day. First period was one of my worst classes. If it would work there, it would work anywhere. I spent that night thinking of what I would say in the morning, rehearsing various scenarios that might unfold.

Morning came all too soon. I was a little nervous about the whole thing. Having had politeness and respect drilled into me by my parents for twenty years, I was not the loud type. Talking in measured, reasoned cadences was how my own family communicated. If we did get mad, we were told to calm down before we said anything that we might later regret. Getting mad in public was just not done. Pretending to be mad would require more acting ability than I felt I had.

The first period bell rang. I took attendance. For a time, it appeared that the opportunity to get mad would not present itself. I needn't have worried. Soon, Martin Adams, my most obnoxious student, had turned around and was talking to the girl behind him.

"I am tired of asking you people to get quiet," I said loudly and angrily. "We waste too much time in here just talking." It became very quiet. Nobody moved. They just waited. Martin waited.

"Now, let's get on with our lesson," I said finally. I was able to continue with the class in relative calm, but by the end of the period, the noise level was creeping back to its pre-outburst volume. I knew that the effect of my "mad" would be temporary at best. I had to ask Old Tom what I had done wrong. I made a point to see him at lunch.

"Did you get mad at the class in general or at Martin in particular?" Old Tom asked in answer to my question.

"Well, I guess at the whole class," I confessed.

"That's your problem," said Old Tom. "You've got to get mad at the kid who acted up. If you don't confront him, no one in the class will respect you."

"But all of my education classes said to avoid confrontations and respect students' privacy," I answered.

"That's all well and good for most students. But a trouble-maker has chosen to misbehave in public, and so you have to discipline him publicly. You don't go looking for trouble, but you have to take charge of your own classroom. It takes courage to do that."

His last sentence cut like a knife. Maybe, deep down, I was just plain afraid of my classes. I had to find out. I told Old Tom I would try again tomorrow. He wished me luck.

First period the next day began with its usual turmoil. I quieted everyone down and began going over the previous night's homework. It wasn't long before someone turned around and started talking. I could have predicted who the culprit would be.

"Martin," I yelled. "What do you think you're doing?"

"I ain't doing nuthin'," he said with a sneer. His head was tilted slightly back, and he looked at me through half-closed eyes. He was the picture of teenage cockiness.

"You're turned around in your seat, you're talking, and you're not paying attention," I said. I was still yelling. I was mad, and I wasn't acting. Martin's attitude made getting angry with him easier than I had thought. "You have been disruptive in here for the last time. Get out in the hall."

"I ain't movin'," he said.

"You will move out in the hall either before or after I call the principal down here," I said much more quietly. "I thought we could settle this without calling in someone else. But it's your choice."

Martin got up slowly and slunk out of the room. I had to check periodically to see that he was still standing in the hall. Each time I looked, I expected not to see him. Surprisingly, though, he stayed there for the remainder of the period.

The rest of the class was as one transformed. They all took notes, raised their hands to answer questions, and got right to work on their homework when the time came. My own blood pressure returned to normal about half way through the period. With about ten minutes left, I went out into the hallway to talk to Martin.

"Do you know why I got mad at you?" I asked him.

"I guess," said Martin.

"Do you know what I expect out of you?"

"Yeah," he said. His eyes were focused on a bulletin board about fifteen feet away.

"Tell me, please."

"Don't turn around, and don't talk."

"Do you think you can do that from now on?"

"Yeah," he said reluctantly. He was still looking at the bulletin board.

"OK," I said. "If you think you can do so without talking, you may go back to your seat and start your homework."

Martin turned and headed for the classroom door. I knew I needed to say something else. I wasn't sure what. I just opened my mouth and hoped for an inspiration.

"Just a minute," I said quietly. I paused and wearily rubbed my eyes while my brain raced to think of what to say. Martin waited.

"Martin," I began again, "I think you have the potential to be a really good student. And, believe it or not, I like you. You're ornery, but I still like you. You just need to show a little of that respect that you so desperately want from me and from everybody else. How about it? Can you meet me half-way?"

For the first time Martin looked me in the eye. His own eyes held the tiniest trace of moisture. He lowered his head and silently nodded a couple of times. I nodded back, and we returned to the classroom.

Martin finished the period without incident. I wish I could say that he was well-behaved for the rest of the year. He wasn't. However, both he and the rest of the class were markedly better than they ever had been. No doubt this was due to their fear of getting into trouble. I can't help thinking, though, that after that day they saw me more as a human being capable of showing emotions and less as a robot just teaching mathematics. My relationship with the class steadily improved. I eventually got to where I looked forward to meeting with them.

Even more incredibly, I really did grow to like Martin. For his part, he always went out of his way to say "hello" to me in the hall whenever he saw me.

I have since learned the art of diffusing potentially volatile situations. I've developed a mildly humorous classroom persona. And I've made my lessons more interesting and student-centered. In short, I have become a better teacher. Still, I occasionally get a one-on-one challenge. When that happens,

I think back to the lessons I learned that day. A teacher has to have the courage to take charge of his classroom. Just as importantly, he has to show his students that he cares about them, even when he's angry with them. *Especially* when he's angry with them.

A little mad does go a long way.

Mary Mary

One of my charges that first year was a girl named Mary O'Brien. She was one of a large family of four girls and numerous boys. The curious thing about the O'Brien girls was that, following an old Irish tradition, they were all named "Mary." They had different middle names and either went by those or by both given names. Mary Colleen, Mary Meghan, and Mary Elizabeth had all been through school before Mary. Since she just went by "Mary," and since she was an O'Brien, I assumed that Mary was not only her first name but her middle name as well. If it wasn't, it should have been, for, as the nursery rhyme went, she could be quite contrary.

Mary was a social creature. She always seemed to be in the middle of any gathering. She didn't like math, wasn't good at it, and felt that she would never understand it. She carved her niche at the center of attention, thus, not by demonstrating her mathematical prowess, but by maintaining about herself a continual state of confusion. She employed numerous props to this end: broken pencils, leaky pens, erasers that irreparably smudged her work, glasses that slipped down her nose, cracked nails, split ends, gum stuck in her braces. She would invariably need to visit the rest room to remedy the catastrophe *du jour*. If the crisis were not deemed restroom-worthy, it would soon be followed by a proclamation never known to fail with a male teacher: "I have a female problem."

On one spring day near the end of the school year, Mary was in a particularly talkative mood. She walked into the room talking and continued to talk as I gave the students their instructions for the period. We were reviewing for the final exam, and I had prepared a list of questions to help them study. Most students found it difficult to concentrate on math while Mary was talking, so I scolded her and moved her seat. Needless to say, that had almost no effect on her "stream-of-consciousness" narrative. In desperation, I took a Band-Aid out of the drawer and, with great ceremony, applied it to her mouth. The talking stopped.

The respite was only temporary. Soon there came a strange noise from Mary. It was not quite a moan and not quite a cry. Her eyes were opened wide, her head was tilting from side to side, and she was trying to talk with her lips taped shut. I think she probably could have talked normally, even with the Band-Aid, but she could hardly pass up the opportunity I had given her to play the semi-silent comic to the rest of the class. I took the Band-Aid off her mouth. She breathed a theatrical sigh of relief. Before she could open her mouth to speak, I sent her to the hall.

The class got to work. I circulated around the room, answering questions, checking problems, and prodding the less motivated to stay on task. Soon, there was a knock on the door. It was Dan Williams, one of the vice-principals.

In his first year as an administrator, Dan was only two or three years older than I was. I think it safe to say that he was as much a novice as an administrator as I was as a teacher. He had latched onto the then popular notion that he needed to be "friends" with all the students. As a consequence, he had a reputation among the staff for being easily taken in by those same students.

"Yes?" I asked.

"I need Mary O'Brien's book," he said.

"Why?" I asked. "She's here in the hall."

I stepped out into the hallway and looked at the spot where Mary had been standing. She was gone.

"She is in my office, and she needs to study for her final exam in math," said Dan.

"Dan," I began, "first of all, she was disrupting my class. I told her to stand in the hall. She has now obviously disregarded my instructions by going to the office to see you."

"I don't care about all of that," he said. "All I know is that girl wants to do well on her exam, and she needs her book to study right now."

"She hasn't been concerned about mathematics the entire year. Why do you think she suddenly wants to study now? It's her way of being the center of attention. No, she had her chance to study today, but she chose to disrupt the entire class with her antics. She needs to know that she is accountable for her actions. I expect you to support my discipline and send her back to the hall outside my room."

"I am not sending her back," he replied, totally dismissing everything I had said. "And furthermore, I want you to give me her book so she can study down in my office."

I am by nature, I believe, a cooperative person, especially with those in authority. I generally obeyed my parents. I was not a rebel in college. I would probably have been a loyalist for King George during the American Revolution. The injustice of Dan Williams' position, however, really bothered me. Why was he supporting this disruptive student instead of one of his own staff members? I decided to take a stand.

"I'm not going to get that book," I said quietly.

"Mark," said Dan, "I'm ordering you to go in that room and get her book." He was starting to get mad.

"Dan," I said, more boldly this time, "if you want that book, you'll have to get it yourself."

Dan Williams was stunned. I guess he was used to getting his way, even though he hadn't been an administrator very long.

He quickly regained his composure, put on a stern face, and strode into the room. He walked over to Mary's desk, the only one unoccupied, and pulled her conspicuously closed book out from under a pile of make-up odds and ends and chewing gum wrappers. He left the room without a word. I knew, though, that I had not seen the last of him that day.

A more experienced teacher would have gone straight to the principal and complained bitterly about being overruled by this young rookie administrator. As I was neither experienced nor all that confident, I simply awaited developments. Big mistake. During my afternoon study hall, I was summoned into the principal's office. Dan Williams was there, naturally, and evidently had been for some time. I don't think that the gloat on his face was only in my imagination.

I sat beside Dan and across the desk from the principal himself. Mr. Mathers was a formidable figure. He was an former teacher and coach. Whether he had ever been an athlete himself was open to question. He was certainly not athletic looking. To say that he had a beer belly was somewhat of an understatement. His ample girth was emphasized by the fact that most of it was above his trousers, giving the impression that he had purchased them many years before and was unwilling to admit that his waist size had changed. He might have been a comical figure had he not totally understood how to consolidate and exercise power. As it was, his size was part of his intimidating aura.

"Mr. Williams tells me that you refused to follow his request to get a student's book," he began. His words were cordial and professional enough. But the tone of his voice was ominously controlled. And it seemed as though the controls could be loosed at any moment.

"I felt his request was unreasonable," I said. "That student had been disruptive. She was supposed to be standing in the hall, not wandering down to Mr. Williams office."

"Even so, you should have followed Mr. Williams instructions," he said. He added very slowly, "I will not have a teacher disobeying one of my administrators!"

There followed several seconds of silence. Mr. Mathers leaned back in his leather chair, stretched his arms, and clasped his hands behind his head.

"You know, Mark," he said, "if you won't cooperate with my administrators, you'll need to look for a school down the road to teach at. Because you won't be teaching here. Is that clear?"

I had heard about the "down the road" speech. I never actually thought I would be at the receiving end of it. My face suddenly felt hot. Perspiration was forming at various locations all over my body. I didn't want to lose my job. At the same time, I didn't want him to know how successful his intimidation had been.

"I guess so," I said. There was no point in arguing further. I left the room. I went back to the math/science office where I related the recent unfolding of events to my colleagues. Their unfettered outrage and comments of support helped me to feel a little better. Still, I was mad at myself for having backed down so quickly on what I felt was a matter of principle.

The following day was the exam. We followed a special exam schedule. All of my algebra classes were tested at the same time, and I had to circulate among five different rooms to give the exam and miscellaneous instructions to the teachers who were monitoring it. I was standing in the doorway to the room where Mary's class was being tested, talking to the exam monitor. A quick glance inside told me that everyone was there except Mary. I was about to tell the monitor that one student was missing when a voice called out from down the hall.

"I'm here. Don't start without me," said the voice. I turned to see a lone figure some distance down the hall kneeling on the floor picking up papers that had just fallen from a tattered folder. Although her face was turned away from me, I knew instantly who it was.

"Hurry up, Mary," I said.

"You, know, it wasn't really my fault that I'm late. My mother forgot to set my alarm, and I ..."

"Mary!" I cut her off. "It doesn't matter. Just take your seat so we can get started."

The monitor started to pass out the exams, and I left to check on my other classes. I returned about fifteen minutes later. The students were busy working on the exam. They had all placed their algebra books on the edge of their desks ready to turn in. I made my way around the room, collecting the books and checking to see that the number on each book matched the student's number in my records. When I got to Mary's desk, I noticed that there was no book.

"Where is your book?" I whispered.

"I don't know," she whispered back. "The last time I remember seeing it was in Mr. Williams' office."

I had to stifle a laugh.

The exam concluded uneventfully. I collected the completed exams from the monitors and, along with the returned books, carted them all back to my room. The long process of grading them could begin. First, though, I had to monitor a colleague's exam. On the way there, I checked my mailbox. In it sat an algebra book. I checked the inside cover for a name. Mary O'Brien.

Although I didn't try to find out who returned the book, I had my suspicions. I knew it wasn't Mary. Whoever returned it not only wished to remain anonymous but also knew full well that Mary had not used it to study for the exam. That person also had to have access to Mr. Williams' office, the last place Mary remembered having her book. The list of suspects was a remarkably short one.

Dan Williams' concern for Mary turned out to be rather ephemeral. He never inquired about her exam grade. Perhaps he sensed that she was doomed to fail it, which she did, sadly, and didn't want to admit that he had pulled out his administrative big guns to help a student who let him down.

In treating a teacher as a day laborer rather than a professional, Mr. Williams and Mr. Mathers had won that battle. Yet they lost the war for that teacher's loyalty and respect. I ended up sticking around for many more years and made a point never to back down when I thought they were wrong about an issue. This turned out to be a true learning experience for me. It was like a training exercise, for I never did take that walk "down the road" to look for another school.

Keeping Time with the Band Director

Administrators were not the only people I had trouble with early in my career. My ability to offend or at least ruffle a few feathers seemed to extend to many quarters.

It was the early seventies, and Bridgeport High School had no soccer team. I had played the game in college and decided to start a team to get more involved with the extra-curricular life of the school. I thought that being a coach would allow me to get to know some of the kids in a non-academic setting.

The school agreed to pay for referees and transportation. We had no other money. We did have one ball, home-made wooden goals, no nets, and hand-me-down uniforms discarded by the basketball team ten years earlier. Even with such humble beginnings, the players were excited about playing this new game, and I was equally enthusiastic at the turnout of twenty-five boys.

Our only real problem, besides the fact that no one could play soccer, was that we didn't have a field. The school's athletic director, accordingly, made arrangements for us to

43

use the band's practice field. It was a barely regulation football-sized field squeezed in between an apartment complex, the town library, the school's bus garage, and the back parking lot of the school. The band had used it for many years, and there were length-wise gullies caused by countless rows of musicians marching up and down the field. A ball passed at right angles to these gullies appeared to be on a roller coaster as it repeatedly traversed these man-made summits and valleys. A ball rolling along one of the gullies would be trapped in it, much like a bowling ball once in the gutter was doomed to finish there. As no one on the team possessed the skill to actually make a pass with the soccer ball, this particular drawback did not seem of great importance.

I was surprised that we actually had the use of the field. The band director, a man named Bill Ferroni, had the reputation of a tyrant who would sooner cut his own throat than cooperate with a colleague. I was concerned that there would be some conflicts, but I didn't feel I could look a gift horse in the mouth. The team was given a two-hour period after school during which time they could use the field.

No one on the team had ever played soccer before. We had to start from scratch. I explained the rules of the game and began to teach the skills of trapping, passing, and shooting. As I had played for only three years in college, it was most definitely a case of the blind leading the blind. We always finished our drills with a scrimmage. The boys enjoyed this. Everything seemed to go well Monday, Tuesday, and Wednesday, our first three days of practice.

Then came Thursday. We were taken by surprise when a couple of students with band instruments ran out onto the field during our scrimmage and stood along one of the grooves. Now in those days, soccer was relatively new and unfamiliar, considered "foreign" by some. There were many rules that my players didn't understand yet. Even the most inexperienced of them, though, knew that there weren't supposed to be musicians on the field during the game.

I was about to ask the band members to wait on the sidelines when twenty more of them seemed to materialize out of thin air and stand along those same grooves. Soon there were sixty or seventy of them. At first we tried to play around them. Inevitably, their continued presence on the field became impossible to ignore. It wasn't long before my players were making no effort to avoid them at all, and often the ball would ricochet off one or more of them. Once I thought the tuba was going to get nailed with a wild ball. Fortunately, he managed to duck just in time.

During all of this there was no sign of the band director. Our allotted time was not up, so I did not feel compelled to relinquish the field. We scrimmaged for another five minutes, and I finally sent the boys into the locker room to change. Still no band director.

My youth, inexperience, and an inbred tendency to be polite prevented me from saying anything to the band members. As I drove home from practice, though, I went over the events of the afternoon in my mind. The more I thought, the angrier I got. How dare that band director send his kids onto the field during our practice time! I was irritated with myself for not being more assertive and running the musicians off the field. I made up my mind to confront the band director at school the next day.

Next morning, I was in the mail room waiting to use the mimeograph machine. I was thinking of what I would say to the band director when I turned around, and there he was. I swallowed hard and walked over to him. When I did speak, I didn't recognize the sound of my own voice. It seemed higher than usual and had a definite quaver. There was no turning back, though.

"Bill," I said, "why were your band members on our field during our practice time?"

I was prepared for an argument. I was not prepared for what ensued.

"Your field?" Bill yelled, though it was more than a yell. It was a shriek. He had instantly turned beet-red and continued to scream at the top of his lungs.

"Your field! That field has been the band practice field for the last fifteen years. No newcomer is going to waltz in here fresh out of college and tell me that my band has to move, especially for a team that plays soccer. That's a foreign sport.

45

It's un-American. I'll run my band onto the field to interrupt soccer practice whenever I please. You just try to stop me!''

I was literally shaking in my shoes. Bill had moved to within inches of my face during his tirade in an effort to physically intimidate me. But I had made up my mind not to back off. I stood my ground and managed to sputter a reply.

"I was practicing during the time allotted to me. I expect you to do the same," I said, still shaking.

"We'll see about that," he said. He turned his back on me and walked off.

Once he was gone, I resumed breathing. So did the couple of other teachers who happened to be in the mail room.

"You really stood up to him," said one encouragingly.

"I'm not sure. I don't think I put up much of a fight," I said, still not able to talk normally.

"Well, don't let it bother you. Bill blows up at somebody about every other day. He usually then feels bad and apologizes later."

True to form, Bill sought me out later that day. I was teaching, and there was a forceful knock at the door. Before I could answer it, Bill had opened it and motioned me into the hall with a curled index finger. Although not thrilled at being beckoned into his presence, I did join him in the hall.

Bill had stepped back into the hall and was waiting for me. He was an imposing figure. He was about six feet tall and thickly built, yet not fat. He was about thirty-five years old, which seemed ancient to my mere twenty-two years, with hair just starting to gray at the temples. Though normally the picture of self-assurance, he was now preparing himself to do something he obviously didn't want to. His head lowered slightly. There was a moment of embarrassed silence. Then he spoke.

"I shouldn't have yelled at you this morning. Hope there are no hard feelings."

I knew what I was supposed to say. I was supposed to say "Oh, that's all right, Bill," and send him on his way with his conscience cleared.

Of course I did tell him that. I also felt the need to head off future conflicts with our shared field while he was in this penitent mood. I asked him about our practice times and whether they were going to work or not.

The mere mention of our area of conflict brought a rush of blood to his face. I thought I was in for another tongue-lashing, but he managed to control himself.

"Don't push your luck," he said.

"I just need to know when we have the field to practice," I said, trying to sound dispassionate.

"Well, I guess the times the athletic director told you are OK," he finally acknowledged.

"Then we can practice there for the full time allotted us?" I asked. I knew I risked another tirade, but I felt that we had to establish the ground rules.

"You will have your entire time slot. But don't be asking for any more," he added. The conversation at an end, he turned and walked down the hall toward the band room.

I felt pretty good. Although still intimidated by him, I felt that I had won a small victory. He had agreed to what I asked. This was, as it turned out, not the last disagreement that Bill and I had over that field. The real irony of the struggle, though, is that the small plot of land over which we battled is now neither a band practice field nor a soccer field. Its ridges are gone. Even its grass is gone. It was paved over several years ago to make way for a set of six tennis courts.

II. Shedding the Rookie Image?
Mr. Fussy

Somehow I made it through those first couple of years. Thanks to the worst of my students, I learned to maintain fairly consistent classroom discipline. I had also moved up the teacher pecking order and taught both geometry and second-year algebra classes. These proved a delight. The students were more advanced than those in Algebra I and much more interested in learning. Further, I discovered a valuable tool that helped not only with classroom management but also with the presentation of the lessons. That tool was humor.

I am ashamed to admit that my first attempts at humor were misdirected. I fell into the trap into which many teachers fall. I picked on my students. Those slow to understand presented such easy targets, and I could always count on getting laughs from the others. I realize now that those laughs were dearly paid for by the loss of trust of more than a few of my students. I must have been as welcome to them as any self-satisfied lout who greets friends and acquaintances with caustic or demeaning remarks. Such patronizing is usually a manifestation of insecurity. My case was no exception.

In my blissful ignorance, I thought my classes were going wonderfully. The students were quiet and well-behaved. I could make them laugh almost at will. I reigned supreme, in control, and doing a whale of a job teaching mathematics, or so I thought.

One day I ate lunch seated next to Wilber Fortnoy. Close to retirement age, "Wib" taught typing and driver's education. He was short, plump, and balding, a quiet, unassuming man. He knew everything about each kid in his classes, from favorite hobby to latest girlfriend or boyfriend. Kids liked him but tended to take advantage of him a little. I didn't know him well, though I had spoken to him often enough. Almost out of the blue, he made what could only be termed a "proclamation."

"You, know, Mark," he began, "you and Bill Ferroni are probably the most feared teachers in the school."

I felt puzzled. Had he said "respected," I would have been very flattered. He hadn't. He had said "feared." He also had paired me with Bill Ferroni, easily the most tyrannical, uncooperative teacher in the building. I was definitely not flattered. Waiting for him to continue, I simply looked in his direction.

"That's neither good nor bad," he said. "That's just your personality."

"Oh," I responded, not knowing what else to say.

Wib had finished his lunch. He excused himself, rose, and left the table. His statement, however, remained with me for the rest of the day and for several days afterward. The more I thought about his comment, the more I was bothered by it.

I began to re-examine my relationship with my classes, especially with the students who never said much. I didn't like what I saw. Most of those who seemed to enjoy the classes were either "A" students who radiated confidence or extroverts who liked the attention I gave them. The others just sat there, averting their eyes, trying not to be noticed. This was not an atmosphere that fostered thoughtful questioning or stimulated academic growth. I knew I had to make some changes.

I began by changing my attitude toward student questions. Instead of viewing them as interruptions to the lessons, I saw them as windows into the minds of my students. Their questions revealed everything from major misconceptions to great insight. I made it extremely easy for them to ask questions and strove to treat each question, even the most elementary one, with the utmost respect. Slowly, the kids started to ask more questions. I felt like I was beginning to reach them. Even the kids who never spoke joined in the discussions, if only with their eyes.

Because I had stopped making fun of wrong answers, however, I lost a major source of my classroom humor. I had to find something to replace it. I stumbled on such a source quite by accident.

I am, by nature, fairly neat and tidy. It is now fashionable to refer to such tendencies as "anal retentive," a less-than-complementary term actually invented, I'm certain, not by Freud, but by some obscure malcontent with a PhD who could never organize his closets. At that time, however, neither being aware of nor caring about the psychological implications of compulsive tidiness, I insisted that my classroom be neat and orderly.

The proper alignment of the students' desks, though, remained a continual thorn in my side. Our desks always seemed to be out of line. Students would pull them toward themselves after they sat down instead of scooting their chairs under the properly positioned tables. Worse yet, they would often push the desks completely out of line as they rose to leave the classroom. More often than not, the room was a mess before the start of any period, having been left that way by the previous class.

I came up with a solution that I thought was both instructive and practical, one worthy of a mathematics teacher. The lines formed by the tiles on the floor would serve as the grid for a two-dimensional, room-size coordinate graph. Every corner of every tile would be assigned an ordered pair of numbers. It would then be simple to put each table leg on the right spot. Students not only would see a practical application of graphing, but also would help me keep the room tidy. We could even break up into small work groups, moving desks about, and still know the exact spots to which the desks must be returned before the period ended. Chairs would, of course, have to be pushed in as students left their desks.

I was surprised at the students' reaction when I told them of my plan. They laughed. I had proposed the idea in all seriousness, but they thought I was joking. Though disconcerted at first, I soon realized that I had discovered that elusive source of classroom humor. Instead of making fun of my students, I would, in effect, poke fun at myself. It worked beautifully. It also launched the development of my own classroom persona. Accordingly, I instituted my desk-alignment plan with enough tongue-in-cheek banter that the students didn't know whether I was totally serious or just trying to have some fun. I thought it best to keep them guessing.

My second-period Algebra II class that year responded well to such humor. One day I noticed a single circle of paper on the floor beside Courtney Phillips' desk. It was tiny, the debris from a paper hole punch she had just been using. I eyed it on the floor and walked slowly toward her desk.

"Oh, Courtney," I said pleasantly, yet with a trace of concern, "someone has left a pile of *rubbish* by your desk. I'm sure it wasn't you, but would you mind taking care of it for me, please?"

Courtney quickly looked at the floor on both sides of her desk. At first, she couldn't see the "pile." When she finally spotted the tiny dot of paper, a smile crept over her previously puzzled face. She leaned over to pick it up. Everyone around her also smiled or quietly chuckled. A few shook their heads in benign disbelief. I think they viewed me in much the same way that Indians during frontier times viewed those white settlers who had gone mad. They gave them a wide berth, believing their craziness to be a special gift from the Great Spirit, and didn't harm them for fear of arousing his displeasure.

Having joined the ranks of the mildly eccentric, I felt a new freedom to experiment even in the way I presented my lessons. I had the kids repeat chants and jingles to help them memorize theorems and tried to think of curious or outlandish analogies that would familiarize obscure geometric or algebraic concepts. One such metaphor, "Grandma's Pet Wolf," described an unusual pet tied to a stake in the back yard and illustrated the idea of the interior and exterior of a circle. The students had to choose locations where it would be safe to lay their tanning blankets and soon realized that the radius of that critical circle was the length of the wolf's chain. "The Blob," yet another teaching ploy, conveyed the idea of substitution. Instead of using a letter to represent an unknown amount, I would draw a large blob on the board every time that amount was needed. Eventually, I would "stamp" the correct letter or expression on all of the blobs using the flat part of my fist as though it were actually printed there. Of course, after hitting the board I would hurriedly have to write the expression on the blob while I still stood directly in front of it, and then dramatically step aside to reveal to my student audience the "substituted" expression. Though they all saw through the obvious "stamping" charade, they also seemed to understand the concept of substitution.

I happened upon one of my most useful techniques in second-period Algebra II that year. Courtney Phillips was having trouble solving equations. That in itself was not unusual. Courtney had trouble with almost everything mathematical. Although an outstanding student in every other course, she struggled profoundly with algebra. She asked at least ten question every period, for which I was glad. It showed me that she felt comfortable in asking them. Further, I knew that when Courtney understood a topic, *everyone* understood it. The rest of the class knew this and exhibited toward her both patience and support. Still, solving equations remained a major stumbling block.

"There are so many things you have to do, so many different rules," she blurted out in frustration one day. "I never know which one to use or where to start."

I had struggled for weeks to get her to understand the process, but with little success. We had compared equations to balance scales in the science lab or even to teeter-totters on the playground. Both were tried and true analogies. Neither had worked for Courtney. On this day, as I actually listened to her plaintive comment, the light suddenly dawned on me. There were too many rules!

I stopped short, formulating my thoughts. The room was silent for a moment. Then I began.

"Courtney, you have to know only two rules to solve equations. The first one," I said, pausing for effect, "is B.S."

In a classroom where inappropriate language could barely be contemplated, much less spoken, these two letters rang out like gunshots. Students sat up and looked at each other with wide-eyed expressions on their faces. A few in the back of the room snickered. I pretended not to notice as I wrote those two letters in gigantic capitals on the board.

"Yes, these two letters form the basis for our work in equations. Does anyone know what they stand for?" I waited a moment. No one spoke. "How about the first one?" I continued. "Does anyone know what the *b* stands for?"

At this question, the snickerers in the back of the room coughed and sputtered, yet dared not speak the word. It was a serious boy in the front row who cautiously raised his hand and quietly ventured, "Bull?"

Tilting my head and giving him a quizzical look, I slowly allowed an expression of comprehension to transform my face. I opened my own eyes wide, registering both shock and disapproval. This scene, incidentally, took every bit of the modest acting ability that I possessed.

"Oh, no!" I exclaimed as twenty-five teenagers finally unleashed their pent-up laughter. When the class settled down, I proceeded to explain.

"The true meaning of B.S. is not what many of you obviously think. It really stands for 'both sides.' The rule says that whatever you do to an equation, you must do it to both sides. Whether you add, subtract, multiply, divide, or even take the square root, you must do that to both sides of the equation."

"The second rule is the 'Undoing Principle.' This tells you *what* to do to both sides. If you're adding three to 'x,' then you subtract three from both sides to get rid of it or undo it. If you are multiplying 'x' by five, then you divide both sides by five to undo that. When you have 'undone' everything that is being done to 'x,' you'll have 'x' by itself and will have solved the equation." We worked through several examples.

"Two simple rules," I concluded, "B.S. and Undoing."

Those who already knew how to solve equations were, by this time, yawning with boredom. Some of the students who had been having trouble were tentatively nodding their heads in agreement. Courtney Phillips, at the center of the maelstrom, sat transfixed, staring at those two giant letters still on the board.

"I think I get it," she finally said. Those five words made my day.

And Courtney did get it. In fact, she blossomed. She still asked just as many questions, maybe more, but her questions revealed insight and took on an air of confidence and authority. She had taken charge of her own education.

At the end of the school year, she gave me a small book. It was an illustrated children's book about a little man who had to have everything just so. He had a perfect little house and even combed the grass in his lawn so that it all faced the same direction. His name was "Mr. Fussy."

"This is for that little dot of paper that you made me pick up at the beginning of the year," she said, smiling. She had already shown the book to just about everyone else in class. They all waited for my reaction.

"Thank you very much, Courtney," I said, leafing through the pages, "but I really don't see what this has to do with me."

My slight smile turned into a grin, and I read the funny little book aloud to the class.

Pythagoras

With each passing year, I discovered more about the art of teaching. Learning techniques that made the job easier and gaining the confidence to implement them, I began to relax and enjoy myself in the classroom. I thought I could probably teach anything, rather like the born salesman who could sell anything, from shoes to used cars. This, of course, was not enough. Form without substance rarely is. I had to have something to say.

It took some time for me to realize what that was. As a math teacher, I knew I must teach students most of the canned procedures in the book. This was mandated by state and local guidelines. I felt, though, that they needed to be able to do more than memorize algorithms. They needed to struggle with difficult problems and use logic along with those algorithms to draw conclusions from apparent chaos. In other words, they needed to think. Now known among educators as "critical" thinking, it used to be called just plain thinking.

Geometry is tailor-made for developing powers of deductive reasoning. Euclid's ancient set of postulates and theorems constituted the first logical mathematical system in the world.

It still serves as the basis for our study of geometry. Perhaps the most famous, most useful theorem of them all is the Pythagorean Theorem. Students can memorize it easily but have trouble understanding why it works or how it can be applied.

As I struggled to make the Pythagorean Theorem understandable, I happened upon a way to present it that was novel, to say the least. My classes that year had wrestled mightily with even the simplest of concepts, so I knew I had my work cut out for me. I sat at home one evening grading their papers and puzzling over new or exciting approaches to teach the Pythagorean Theorem. Just as I began to nod off, the telephone rang.

"Hi, *Kauch*," said the voice at the other end. It was Ted Bishop. Ted was a fellow soccer coach and history teacher from a neighboring school district. He always greeted me by imitating a certain foreign-born high school soccer referee who had a very distinctive way of pronouncing the word *coach*.

"Hi, Ted," I said. "What's up?"

I was glad to hear from him, but I knew that I would be spending the next forty-five minutes on the phone. Ted was a prolific talker. I settled back in my chair to get comfortable.

After Ted had relayed all the important soccer news and information, he moved on to school-related topics: administrators who were useless, colleagues who couldn't teach, and the myriad of students who were too lazy to learn anything.

"You know what I even did today?" he finally said. I didn't even get a chance to say *no* before he answered his own question.

"I was U.S. Grant," he proclaimed, pausing for effect.

"What do you mean?" I asked.

"I mean I was U.S. Grant," he said again, thinking that a loud and emphatic repetition constituted an explanation.

"What exactly do you mean?" I repeated. Two could play at that game.

"I dressed up as U.S. Grant to present his life and times. I had a whole monologue memorized and presented it as though I were relating my memoirs. I had a beard and everything. It was great."

"It sounds great," I echoed.

56

"But, you know, there were kids who didn't appreciate it. I even had one 'low-life' sleep through it. Sometimes I wonder why I work so hard. These kids just don't know what we go through to prepare interesting lessons. They sit there and complain about being bored when all they need is for someone to give them a good kick in the backside. I blame their parents, but don't get me started on that!"

The last thing I wanted was to get Ted "started," though it seemed he already was. He continued his diatribe for another ten minutes, touching on numerous other topics. His final complaint was over the amount of time he had to spend on the phone because of his various school and soccer commitments. As a result, he never seemed to finish his grading. He finally said good-bye.

It had been a rather long forty-five minutes. Amidst all his complaining and gossiping, though, Ted had given me a way to stamp the Pythagorean Theorem indelibly onto the minds of my students. I would become Pythagoras!

The more I thought about it, the more excited I got. I checked books out of the library on Pythagoras, Euclid, and other ancient mathematicians. I would not merely explain the famous theorem to my classes. I would dazzle them with historical data about Pythagoras' life and times.

The costume and make-up would be a problem. For help I turned to the minister at our church. He had given a series of sermons portraying Biblical characters for which he made his own costumes. He was delighted to help me, but I swore him to secrecy. No one was going to know about Pythagoras ahead of time.

On the day of the presentation, Pastor Silvers met me at my room an hour before school started. He had the costume and make-up. The costume consisted of a white bed-sheet-turned-toga and a folded bed sheet dyed red which served as a sash. I had nothing which resembled ancient shoes, so an old pair of rubber thongs had to do. Before I could put any on of this, I had to have the make-up applied.

We used a large book-storage closet next to my room so that we could get ready without being observed by any students. Pastor Silvers turned out to be an expert at stage make-up. He started with the beard. He had pulled several clumps of gray "hair" out of a braided strand of the same material. In the strand it looked like rather stout gray rope. Pulled apart, stretched, and ironed, it turned into something you might expect to see on the floor of a barber shop. He had several of these hair sections and glued them individually to my face in layers. It gave the beard a very realistic look. He added wrinkles, sprayed-on gray hair, and a sickly pallor which would convey my extreme age.

Once the make-up was complete, I put on the toga and sash. Pastor Silvers pronounced the costume a success and wished me luck in the presentation. I thanked him, and he hurried off to church.

I had a few minutes to look over my notes on Pythagoras, which I had to memorize. The real Pythagoras would hardly have to look at notes to talk about his life or his theorem. I felt pretty confident as I thought about what I would say. I was determined that this would be a dramatic triumph.

I had previously arranged to have Jim Novotny, the teacher across the hall, introduce "Pythagoras" to each of my classes throughout the day. He knew where I was getting ready and surreptitiously knocked on the book room door.

"Meuser," he whispered, "you in there?"

"Yeah," I said. "Come on in."

"You gotta be kidding!" he blurted out as he got his first look at my outfit.

"Don't you like it?" I asked, somewhat taken aback.

"No, it's fine," he said, recovering his composure.

"Now, you'll take my attendance for me. And then explain that I am not here today but that we have a guest speaker who just arrived from Greece. Then announce me as Pythagoras. Got it?"

He nodded.

"Thanks a lot. I really appreciate your help."

Though I was glad for Jim's assistance, I was a little concerned at his reaction to my costume. If he reacted as he did, the kids might react in the same way, or worse. My vision of an inspiring presentation was starting to fade. For the first time, I had doubts about the wisdom of dressing up in a bed sheet in front of twenty-five teenagers.

The bell rang. From my hiding place in the closet, I could hear my friend quiet the class and take attendance. Then he started the explanation of my absence and the introduction of Pythagoras. I was getting more nervous as the moment of truth neared.

"And here is your guest speaker, Mr. Pythagoras," Jim concluded. He quickly left the room.

I walked in. For a split second there was stunned silence. Then, as if on cue, twenty-five voices broke out in spontaneous laughter. Students were literally rolling in the aisles. One student was pounding his desk with the flat of his hand several times. His head was tilted back, mouth open wide. He emitted a long, loud cry of laughter, punctuated by several short staccatos at the end. He took a breath, looked at me a second time, and began his entire laughing litany anew.

The laughter from all over the room continued for what seemed an eternity. I thought I would never get control of the class. All I could do was to start talking and hope for the best.

"Yes, my name is Pythagoras," I said above the din. "Mr. Meuser picked me up at the airport this morning, but he had car trouble, so I came over in a cab. He was sorry he couldn't be here. If he gets his car fixed, he'll be along soon."

I never did admit to being myself. I stayed in the Pythagoras character and started talking about his birth, his life, and his almost cult-like following. Strangely enough, the class settled down and listened.

Pythagoras, I discovered in my research, originated the idea of the secret society. He formed a band of loyal followers known as the Society of the Pythagoreans. It may have been one of them who actually proved the famous theorem. The Pythagoreans were not only interested in mathematics, but also in mysticism. They attributed strange and magical powers to certain numbers. Many traditions of modern-day secret societies trace their roots to the Pythagoreans. They also took their membership quite seriously. One of their number was killed for divulging a mathematical secret to the general public.

Once I had set the stage, I was ready for the Pythagorean Theorem itself. I had to use a few geometric principles that we had been discussing earlier that week. On the board I drew a right triangle. I then drew the altitude to its hypotenuse, or longest side, forming two more right triangles.

"Who can tell me which triangles are similar?" I asked, referring to the figure on the board. Several hands went up.

"Adam," I said, calling on one of the first hands raised but not realizing that Pythagoras would not have known Adam's name. Adam answered the question correctly and then had a question of his own.

"How did you know my name?" he asked slowly, with just a trace of a smirk. It was enough to catch everyone's attention, and they all waited to see if I could get out of this blunder.

"Uh," I stammered, glancing from side to side, "the great and wise Pythagoras knows all." I said this slowly and loudly, sounding a little like the Wizard of Oz after the drawn curtain revealed him to be a mere mortal.

The class loved it. Teenagers, after all, are more impressed with stand-up comedy than with careful research or thoughtful insight. From this point on, they found it fun to play along with my Pythagoras character. As we worked through the geometrical proof of the theorem, I complimented them on their mathematical prowess when they answered questions correctly. I also told them that they must have a wonderful teacher because they knew so much about geometry.

"You young people don't realize what you have these days," I said after we finished the proof. "You have things we never dreamed of: things like paper, and pencils, and chalk. Why, I've heard there is even a little machine that can add and subtract for you if you just hit a few buttons!"

"Yes, we have just all sorts of things nowadays, Mr. Pythagoras," said a girl in the front row. "You know, you say a lot of the same things Mr. Meuser does. Are you sure the two of you aren't related?"

Everybody laughed.

"I don't think so," I said. "But, he sounds like a really fantastic teacher. I wish he could have joined us today."

"I'm just as glad he wasn't here," said Adam. "That car trouble he had today was, in my opinion, just payback for all the hard tests he has given us."

"I really don't know about that, young man," I said, lowering one eyebrow and giving him a sharp look. "You'll have to take that up with him when he returns tomorrow.

"Now that I have shown you my famous theorem, I would like to share with you something very special yet little known. Everyone knows about the Society of the Pythagoreans. Not everyone knows about a group closely affiliated with the Pythagoreans. It was our ladies' auxiliary, a singing and dancing troop made up of the wives of the Pythagoreans, called the 'Pythagorettes.' I would like to close by singing for you one of their most-requested songs."

I walked over to the closet in the room and pulled out a banjo which I had secreted there. The song I performed was to the tune of "She'll be Comin' Round the Mountain."

"Oh, the sum of the squares of the legs

Is the square of the old hypotenuse.

Now, don't you forget it. Now, don't you forget it.

'Cause that's the theorem of Pythagoroos (sic)."

I finished the song with a big chord strummed on the banjo. It was followed by fairly enthusiastic applause from my student audience. I bowed, thanked them, wished them good luck in their geometrical studies, and bade them a fond farewell.

I quickly scurried out of the room and into the nearby book room, nearly collapsing onto its only chair. Well, I thought, that wasn't too bad. It had gone nothing like I had expected. I had, of course, visualized myself as an actor portraying an ancient mathematician. Instead, I was more of a comedian, going for laughs and sneaking in a bit of geometry here and there. What could I expect, dressed as though I were headed for a fraternity toga party?

The bell to change classes rang. One down, and four to go. I hoped my beard and make-up would hold up throughout the day through all the sweat. I dabbed a little at my face.

Jim Novotny peeked in the door.

"How'd it go? Ready for another one?" he asked.

"It went pretty well after the initial shock wore off. I'm not sure I'm ready for the next class, though. I really don't have much choice at this stage, do I?"

"No," he said. "I'll get my kids settled down and come over and introduce you again."

The rest of the day went well. I added little bits to the monologue and relaxed more each successive period, making sure to include the blunder of calling a supposedly unknown student by name. I always had someone catch me on it and each time got a laugh with my pat answer. Still, I was truly thankful when the last chord of the banjo rang out in the last class of the day. Once back in the book room, I literally ripped the beard off my face. It itched horribly by this time. I put on street clothes, packed up my banjo, toga, and lecture notes, and headed for home where a soothing shower awaited me.

Pythagoras was the talk of the school for days. I asked my students the next day how our "guest speaker" had been. Most thought the speaker had done pretty well. A few thought he was much too old to be on the lecture circuit. Still others thought he was absolutely out of his mind. They were careful to say this about Pythagoras and not about me, but the veiled implication was clear. Nevertheless, they did seem to understand his theorem and did a reasonable job of applying it to a variety of situations. If the presence of Pythagoras had motivated them to think "critically," then perhaps it had been worth all the effort.

A couple of weeks later, I got a call from Ted Bishop.

"Hi, *Kauch*," he said, instantly yet namelessly identifying himself. "How are you?"

"I'm fine," I answered, and before he could respond, I did something that I almost never did while on the phone with Ted. I made an unsolicited comment. "I was Pythagoras."

"What are you talking about?" he asked, somewhat taken aback that I had grabbed the lead in our conversation.

"I dressed up as Pythagoras in my geometry classes to present the Pythagorean Theorem. It actually went pretty well, if I do say so myself."

"That's great. Did I tell you that I did another historical character? William McKinley. He is the most underrated president in the bunch. I really worked hard on this one, and, wouldn't you know, there were a couple of kids who fell asleep in the back row. I don't know why I put up with those kids. It just shows you that . . ."

I sighed inwardly and settled back in my chair to get comfortable.

A Window of Opportunity

Despite my growing confidence in the classroom, I still occasionally wondered why anyone in his right mind would want to be a teacher. Unruly students, uncooperative parents, endless grading, and oceans of forms and red tape posed but a few of the problems to be tackled. Yet these difficulties paled when compared with those faced by the unsung heroes of the teaching profession, without whose daily help the entire operation of any school would come to a grinding halt. I refer, of course, to substitute teachers. To understand their plight, one should imagine facing a classroom full of unknown teenagers and trying to get them to work on something that neither they nor you understand completely. It has to be a challenge, to say the least. Still, subs do it every day and manage to get through it fairly uneventfully. One incident comes to mind, however, that was anything but uneventful.

On this occasion, I was attending a mathematics conference, and an older lady, Mrs. Virginia Peters, was hired as the substitute. I had made plans for her that should have kept the students busy the entire period. I left it up to her whether or not students could work in groups on the assignment. She had evidently allowed them to do so in the first three periods, so she felt comfortable in doing the same for fourth period. She did not know, however, that on fourth period's roster was one of my all-time great class comedians, Todd Meecham.

Todd was a smart boy. He had a sizable lazy streak so his grades weren't all that impressive. Yet he had a very analytical mind. He also had a well-developed sense of humor. He was genuinely funny but always managed to laugh with people rather than at them. The only time I remember Todd not laughing was when he was in a hospital bed after undergoing stomach surgery. He said that the doctor had specifically told him not to laugh, or the stitches would rip out. Even so, he managed a couple of small chuckles while I was there.

On this day, however, he was in fine form. The atmosphere in the fourth period classroom was relaxed, with students moving from table to table, ostensibly comparing solutions, but probably catching up on the latest gossip. Todd enlisted the aid of a confederate, whose identity I never did learn. While his confederate went to Mrs. Peters' desk and occupied her with a particularly difficult problem, Todd slipped out of the room. The room was on the second floor, and he quickly made his way down the stairs and out the front door. He carefully lay down in the grass just below the bank of windows in my room. His arms were outstretched, one slightly ahead of the other.

It was spring, and all the windows of the room were open wide. Back in the room, Todd's confederate left the teacher's desk and walked over to the window directly above Todd. With all the theatrical acumen that he could muster, he called out, "Todd's fallen out of the window!"

"What?" Mrs. Peters queried, not wanting to be taken in by a teenage prank.

"No, really. You've got to get some help!" the confederate persisted. His voice sounded urgent.

She was still unconvinced. By this time, though, several other students had gathered at the window. They were talking and shouting so much that she felt obligated to at least get up and corral them back to their seats. She made her way to the crowd at the window and looked out. There on the ground below was Todd's lifeless form sprawled on the grass!

"Get an ambulance! Call the principal," she screamed. The once-calm room was now pandemonium. Only a couple of students were in on Todd's stunt. Most of the others, like Mrs. Peters, thought that he was lying gravely injured on the lawn.

"I'll go to the office!" shouted the confederate.

Other students helped poor Mrs. Peters into a chair, for she was visibly shaken. She was just beginning to muster the strength to get up from the chair, for she felt that she herself should go to the office, when Todd's smiling face appeared at the classroom door. He walked sheepishly over to her.

"I didn't want you to have a heart attack," he said.

"Well, you very nearly gave me one, young man," she said. Though her tone was reproachful, she was, in fact, very relieved. Sprinkles of laughter emanated from various locations around the room as groups of students still standing there realized what Todd had done. Even Mrs. Peters was shaking her head and smiling as she slowly walked back to her desk.

The room returned to normal, although little mathematics was done for the remainder of the period. Todd was the hero of the hour. Everyone else wished that he had thought of such a "clever" stunt. Todd knew, though, even as he basked in his momentary glory, that the day of retribution would come. It was Friday, and he would be safe through the weekend. However, come Monday morning, he thought, Mr. Meuser would be back, and Mr. Meuser would not be pleased.

I returned Monday morning from the conference enthused with several good ideas that I wanted to try out that week. I was faced with the paperwork of my absence: forms from the office to fill out and papers with Friday's class work to grade. Among the pile of papers was the substitute's report. I glanced at it. Nothing out of the ordinary. The usual compliments on the well-behaved classes she had had on Friday. I set it aside.

My first three classes were predictable. I told them about the conference and asked how everything had gone on Friday. All was in order. Then came fourth period. I told them about the conference and again asked how things went in my absence. The ensuing silence was palpable. It soon gave way to barely audible chuckling and furtive, sideways glances. It didn't take a genius to figure out that something was up.

"All right, what happened?" I asked.

Again, silence.

I pressed the issue. "If something happened, you know I will find out about it. You might as well tell me yourselves," I said.

Finally, Todd Meecham spoke up. "You have to promise that you won't get mad," he said.

"I can't make that promise, Todd. If something bad happened, I will have to deal with it."

"Have you read the substitute's report, yet?" he asked. I could see the wheels turning in his head. He was hoping Mrs. Peters hadn't mentioned in her report whatever it was that he had done.

"I glanced at it briefly," I said, trying not to convey the fact that there was nothing incriminating in it.

Todd hesitated, then made the plunge. "We played a little trick on her," he admitted. A faint smile played across his face. He went on to tell the whole story.

After he finished, he waited to see what punishment I would exact. The rest of the class waited, too. I thought for a moment. By this time, my reputation as a disciplinarian was secure. I didn't *need* to do anything. And it was such a funny prank. But a prank it was, and if the substitute teacher had reported it, it would have to be dealt with.

"Let's see what the substitute's report says," I said, stalling for time.

I got it off the desk and started reading. "All classes went fine. You have some great classes, especially period four." That settled it.

"Ladies and gentlemen, Todd," I began, "if the substitute teacher did not wish to press the issue any further, then far be it from me to do anything different. Case dismissed."

From that moment on, Period Four and I had a special relationship. There are class personalities that are light and humorous or, at the other end of the spectrum, resentful and hostile. That day Period Four became one of those rare classes that exude warmth and acceptance. Perhaps it was because I had accepted them and their class clown. Whatever the reason, I had Todd to thank for bringing it about.

I saw Todd years later. He had been to college, dropped out, and re-enrolled. He was finally studying to be, of all things, a teacher, and he wanted to stop by my room to see me. He was hopeful that he could do his student teaching at Bridgeport. As it turned out, that did not happen. I asked him about his famous "window of opportunity," and, of course, he remembered it. He laughed with the same youthful laugh of his high school days. There was something about his easy-going demeanor that told me that this class clown would make a great teacher. Sometimes, I thought, the torch is passed to those who seem least likely to receive it.

If there is any justice in this world, though, Todd will have to do a bit of substituting before he gets his first teaching assignment.

Trailblazers of America

"You can't miss it," he said. "You just can't miss it."

A vague feeling of apprehension crept over me as I heard these words. Our soccer team was scheduled to play Liberty High School, in Wheeling, West Virginia, in one week. They had traveled to Bridgeport to play us last year, and it was our turn to reciprocate. I had called the coach to get directions and finalize last-minute details. Reading from the notes I had just taken, I repeated the directions to him. For some reason, he felt compelled to make his fateful pronouncement yet a third time.

"You really can't miss it," he said emphatically.

I thanked him, told him we were looking forward to the game, and said good-bye.

Our team that year was a good one, perhaps the best I have coached. They were undefeated at that point in the season and went on to win the league championship. Like all good teams, they were an ornery bunch. They would have to be supervised carefully on the Wheeling trip, especially since it was our "overnighter." We were to play the game in the afternoon and then spend the night in Wheeling at a motel.

69

By this time, Bridgeport's high school soccer program had grown from one team to three, a varsity, a reserve, and a freshmen team. Although only the varsity team went on the overnighter, all the coaches were needed to help with the trip. Bob Crawford, my varsity assistant, and Tony Michaels, the reserve coach, were to drive the school district's two vans that we had reserved. I preferred not to drive on these trips. Without that responsibility, I could relax a bit before the game during the long ride there. The freshmen coach was also not driving, but for an entirely different reason.

Phil Richmond was the freshmen coach. He was an outgoing man about thirty-five years old. Though still young, he was beginning to take on the comfortable, lived-in look of middle age. His hair was both graying and thinning. He had started to develop a bit of a paunch but steadfastly refused to either exercise or diet. He subscribed to the nineteenth century view that a large midsection on a man was an indication of prosperity. Further, he felt that, in life, it was futile to fight either nature or time. He had decided, rather, that he was going to enjoy himself along the way. He usually did have a good time and was fun to be with, but he was a better leader than follower. In fact, if he happened not to be in charge of a particular activity, he would take delight in mildly sabotaging all or part of that activity.

Phil had actually volunteered to drive. I had told him cordially but firmly that Bob and Tony would be driving. There was a good reason for this. Phil was not a good "caravan" driver. If he drove the lead van, he would invariably speed ahead and lose the second van. If he happened to be driving the second van, he would lag behind until he was out of sight of the lead van. The lead van would then have to slow down until Phil finally caught up. He always claimed never to do any of this on purpose, nonchalantly shrugging off any suggestion of skulduggery.

Game day arrived, and we all gathered at the high school to load kids and equipment into the vans. State guidelines governing the number of passengers allowed in school vans were not yet on the books. So we packed eighteen players, two managers, four coaches, uniforms, balls, equipment, and personal possessions into the two twelve-passenger vans. It was a tight fit, but everyone seemed fairly comfortable and ready for the two-hour trip. As I checked off the names on the team roster to make sure everyone was there, I noticed a bit of confusion in the front of the other van.

To my horror and annoyance, I saw Bob get out of the driver's seat and walk around to the passenger side of the van. Then Phil slid from the passenger's seat to the driver's without even getting out of the van. He did this, I feel certain, to avoid detection.

I finished accounting for all the kids. I then walked over to the other van. Phil was calmly sitting behind the wheel but carefully avoiding looking in my direction.

"What are you doing?" I asked him, making little effort to conceal my astonishment.

"I'm just sitting here," Phil said pleasantly.

"You know what I mean," I said, becoming more exasperated. "Bob is supposed to be driving."

"Oh," he said, pausing slightly as he thought of a good excuse. "Um, Bob didn't sleep real well last night. He didn't feel it would be safe for him to drive, being as tired as he is."

"Is that right?" I asked Bob.

He merely nodded. I half expected him to rub his eyes and yawn to complete the bit of extemporaneous theater that I was witnessing.

"Well, I guess we have no choice. You'd better take the lead. Just make sure that you get only a couple of car lengths ahead of our van. OK?"

"Got it," said Phil, nodding once with great sincerity.

We closed the van doors, waved good-bye to the few parents that were still in the parking lot, and pulled onto Broadview Boulevard, Bridgeport's main thoroughfare, heading for the freeway. All went well for the mile or so that we were on Broadview. As soon as we entered the freeway, however, Phil's van began to pull away from ours.

"He's at it again!" I exclaimed to Tony. "Can you keep up with him?"

"I've got the pedal on the floor already," said Tony.

71

"Why do we always get the slower van?" I loudly asked no one in particular.

Tony muttered something about rotten luck, and we settled resignedly into our seats as Phil's van disappeared over the next rise. I consoled myself with the fact that, with Phil in the lead instead of trailing, we would at least get to Wheeling in good time. As it turned out, we needed every minute of time that we gained from Phil's heavy foot.

The trip in our van was routine. The kids listened to radios, played cards, or just slept. A couple of them helped me with the crossword puzzle from the paper. As we neared Wheeling, I got out my directions. Liberty's game field was in a city park, and there were no facilities in which to change. The plan was for the kids to change into their uniforms at the motel and then go back to the park to play the game. We passed the exit to the city park. I began carefully counting the number of exits so we could simply re-trace our steps when we headed back for the game.

At the third exit past, we saw the sign for our motel and got off the freeway. We arrived in the motel parking lot to find Bob and Phil relaxing by their van, each with a cola in hand. Their kids were exploring the parking lot or sitting in the shade. A couple of them were kicking a soccer ball back and forth.

"Thanks for staying in view," I said sarcastically.

"Oh, did we get ahead of you," said Phil with all the pretense of innocence. "Bob and I got to talking, and we didn't realize that you weren't still behind us."

"Huh," I said. "I would have thought that Bob would have used the trip to catch up on his sleep."

For once Phil didn't have a ready answer.

"I really was tired, but I just couldn't sleep," Bob ventured, trying to rescue his temporarily speechless partner. It was a pretty feeble excuse, but I let it pass. It was enough that they knew that we knew that the sleep-deprivation story was a sham. There was no need actually to say it. From then on, however, our van was to lead. We had the directions to the field, and they would have no choice but to keep up with us.

We walked into the motel lobby to register and check into our rooms. The lobby was basically a long narrow corridor with the motel restaurant entrance in the middle and the check-in desk at one end. At the other end was the strangest thing I have ever seen in a motel lobby. Standing against one wall was the entire cab, hood, and front grill of an old Mack truck, complete with the silver dog hood ornament. We all stood looking at it in amazement for several seconds when the grill suddenly swung open and a man came walking out of what should have been the engine. As the man walked away, the grill swung back into its original position.

It was Bob who walked over to it and gave the grill a tug. It opened to reveal an entire room on the other side. The room was dark and had an other-worldly aura. For a moment, Bob was poised on the brink, contemplating stepping "through the looking glass." He finally took a step inside and disappeared into the darkness. The grill swung closed.

Before we could contemplate his fate or follow him in, the grill opened again. It was Bob, and he was smiling.

"It's a bar," he said, chuckling.

We all laughed. But I realized that we would have to make sure that none of the kids went exploring behind the grill of the Mack truck.

We checked in, assigned rooms, and distributed the keys. The players changed into their uniforms, and we were soon ready to leave for the game. We headed back toward the city park, re-entering the freeway. Our van took the lead, and Phil managed to stay right behind us. I carefully counted the number of exits and had Tony pull off on the third one. I did not realize, though, that there was an extra east-bound exit between the city park exit and the motel. We should have gone on for one more exit. As careful as I thought I had been, we were doomed from the moment we left the freeway.

Directions in hand, I counted streets and traffic lights, turning left or right at the supposedly appropriate times. Nothing seemed to fit. None of the street names matched my directions. Still, we persevered. We eventually found ourselves on a gravel road in a rather seedy section on the outskirts of town. A large creek ran along one side of the road, and on the other stood run-down apartments with missing doors and torn curtains blowing out of the windows. Small children with T-shirts but no shorts or underwear were playing near the road. The gravel road worsened and then just simply stopped. We were at a dead-end. It was, by now, obvious to all that we were hopelessly lost.

I knew that the game field was in the main city park. So after we departed the neighborhood of half-naked children, we stopped to ask directions.

"Yeah, I can get you to the city park," said a friendly-looking man whose smile exposed several missing teeth. "Take this road east for four lights. Turn left, then go about a mile and turn right. You can see the park from there. You can't miss it."

I thanked him. But his last four words, I knew, spelled disaster. Sure enough, we were soon at the end of his directions and no closer to our destination. By now it was the time that our players should have been taking the field and warming up. My consternation had turned to outright panic. We stopped again, this time on a little side street off a well-traveled road.

I saw someone on the other side of the road. I got out of the van and called to him for help. We were on opposite sides of the road, so it was hard for us to hear each other. As there wasn't that much traffic, we met at the double yellow line in the middle of the road so he could give me a clear set of directions. This time I felt confident in the directions. I returned to the vans to find everyone doubled over in laughter. At first I assumed that they were amused at my state of panic. Although they were, that was not the reason for their laughter.

On the side street where we were parked was a neighborhood bar. As I had passed it on my way to the main road, a patron of the bar had come out and taken a few unsteady steps. He heard me call to the man across the main road and followed as best he could, perhaps thinking there was some impending emergency. When my direction-giver and I both walked to the middle of the road, it was too much excitement for him. As he stood watching us, feeling certain that we were going to be killed at any second, a dark stain began to form on one of his pant legs. Soon it was a rather large, dripping stain. Some of the moisture found its way to the sidewalk.

To high school students, this was the funniest thing they had ever seen. They told and re-told the story to each other several times before the game. I never actually saw the man but found out what happened only through their stories.

We finally made it to the city park and to the game. We arrived just as the Liberty players were setting up the field, so we still had time to spare. After the game began, it soon became obvious that they were not as skilled a team as we were. Even though we dominated play, however, we just couldn't seem to score. It was only in the last five minutes that Jimmy Price, our leading scorer, put one in the net to preserve our hitherto unblemished record. We all knew that we were lucky to come away with a victory. It was apparent that none of our players had his mind on the game.

We returned to the motel, and the players showered and got ready for dinner. During this time, Phil and Bob volunteered to make sure that no student ventured near the Mack truck bar. I suspected that they carried out this duty from the other side of the grill door.

The night was a short one. We caught Jimmy Price throwing a waste basket full of water on another player's bed. For that infraction, Jimmy spent the night on the floor of the coaches' room with a blanket and pillow. We got to bed shortly after midnight. Though curfew for the players was also midnight, many of them undoubtedly were awake well past that. The only player whom I know got a good night's sleep was Jimmy.

With some prodding, we were all up by eight the next morning, breakfasted at nine, and on the road by ten. I insisted that Phil's van follow ours for the return trip. He acquiesced without so much as a word. In fact, he had been remarkably quiet on the whole topic of my getting lost. I had expected a whole series of jokes and innuendoes at my expense. There had been nothing. I was a little concerned. It was not like Phil to let such a golden opportunity pass without teasing me just a little.

We were not long on the freeway before Phil's van started to lag behind. This time, I wasn't waiting for him. I asked Tony to keep our speed right at the limit. Soon Phil's van was again visible in our rear-view mirror. He must not have wanted to spend any more time on this trip than he had already.

We arrived back at the high school a little after noon. The kids were, by this time, walking zombies. Those who had parked their cars in the school lot drove home while the others called their parents to pick them up. We coaches returned the vans to the bus garage, made sure the managers got all of the equipment back to the locker room, and waited for the last few parents to collect their boys. At last we were ready to go home, and I was glad to close the book on another over-nighter. As I was soon to discover, this book was not yet ready to be closed.

Our end-of-season banquet was held in early November. Having won our league championship, we wanted to make this banquet special. It was a pot luck affair. Each player's family provided food, the quality and quantity of which was worthy of the occasion. Once the meal was finished, the awards for all three teams were presented. The tributes to all three squads, especially the varsity, were glowing. Many team and league awards were conferred. Jimmy Price was awarded the MVP trophy.

It was all starting to wind down. I had a very self-satisfied feeling. We had won our league championship for the first time. We had been ranked first in our area by several coaches' polls. I had even been selected as "Coach of the Year" for our league. Except for a disappointingly early loss in the state tournament, it had been a dream season. I savored the moment but was glad for the free time that the end of the season would bring. I think I even breathed an audible sigh.

The captains spoke last. When they were done, instead of thanking everyone and wishing them a "good night," they said that there was one more speaker.

Phil Richmond rose and walked to the podium. He carried something in a paper bag.

"We have one more award to present," he said. "Coach Meuser, would you come up here, please."

I walked slowly and warily to the podium.

"It is true that this has been our best season ever," he said. "The same cannot be said about this year's overnighter."

He went on to tell the whole story of my getting lost, from the touring the run-down sections of Wheeling to the drunk losing control of his bladder. Phil told the story well, adding embellishments where necessary, and the audience was near hysteria at several points in his narrative.

He concluded by presenting me with an award he had made and framed. It read as follows: "Trailblazers of America presents to Coach Meuser the 1983 pathfinders award for cultural exploration of West Virginia."

All the jokes and material that he could have used that day in Wheeling he saved for his presentation at the banquet. Of course he mentioned my insistence on being in the lead van, for all the good that did. While it was true that Phil was having fun at my expense, he did it good-naturedly. I'll have to admit that I was laughing as hard as everyone else as the story unfolded. The award itself had taken quite some time to fashion and frame. I really did appreciate it.

As it turned out, "Trailblazer" was the only tangible award I received that season. In those days, neither the league championship nor the Coach of the Year award came with any certificate or plaque. "Trailblazer," therefore, hangs in a prominent place on my study wall. That makes it impossible for me to think about what was probably my best season as a coach without coming face-to-face with that more humbling reminder of my own shortcomings.

I have also come to the conclusion that no one ever says, "You can't miss it," unless you can.

III. An English Education: Not All Tea and Crumpets
Welcome to Tilbury

The meeting could have taken place at any educational institution in the English-speaking world. I sat shoulder-to-shoulder with fellow teachers barely listening to an administrator drone on about something virtually inconsequential. A quick glance at my neighbors' slowly nodding heads revealed that they were similarly engrossed. I had attended scores of such meetings. Only one fact made this one unique for me: its location was at Tilbury High School, just outside of Liverpool, England.

As I sat there desperately trying to pay attention, my thoughts drifted back to the beginnings of my English odyssey. It had been over a year since I had applied to teach in Britain through the Fulbright Teacher Exchange Program, a government-sponsored program facilitating year-long exchanges between American teachers and teachers from all over the world. Though brimming with thousands of U.S. applicants, the program had fewer than two hundred English ones. Positions were scarce. It was evidently my combination of math and soccer that enabled me to match up with Steven Pierce, a teacher at Tilbury.

We had arranged for Steven to live in our home during his stay in Bridgeport, and he reciprocated by providing my wife Susan and me with a lovely house in the picturesque village of Thornby Heath, located about fifteen miles from Tilbury. It was a typical northern English village, with a small Anglican church and smaller-still Methodist church, a green grocer, two pubs, a few small shops, and a nice restaurant. By far its most popular gathering place, though, was the local British Legion Hall, where we were to spend many an evening in the company of friends. Though Liverpool itself was somewhat depressed economically, Thornby Heath appeared largely untouched by the problems of its big-city neighbor. The only exception to this was an occasional burglary, when youths from Liverpool would ride the train to Thornby Heath, rob a few isolated houses while their occupants were at work, ride the train back, and probably stop by a pub for a "pint" after their hard day's work. Luckily, we never had to deal with that.

Susan and I spent three weeks settling into our new home. We bought a used car and did as much sight-seeing as we could. We also mowed the lawn regularly and clipped and pruned our somewhat unkempt garden. In a country where gardening is a national passion, this apparently put us in good stead with our hitherto reserved and almost invisible neighbors. By the time school started, we had made quite a few friends. I could have spent the year gardening, sight-seeing, and meeting people, but I did have to teach. This, after all, was why we were here.

At the opening-day meeting at school, I truly did try to stay awake. Miss Wimbish, the head teacher, or principal, did most of the talking. She seemed at first to be very professional and to the point. She did have the habit of putting on and taking off her glasses rather more than necessary. In fact, she did it so often that it appeared to be more of an affectation than a real need to see or not to see. As I became more distracted by her glasses than I should have, I paid less attention to what she was saying and wandered into my pleasant reverie. I was jolted back to attention by her mention of my home town.

79

"... and coming to us all the way from Bridgeport High School in the United States, is Mark Meuser. He is taking Steven Pierce's place this year. Mr. Meuser, would you stand, please?"

I stood and smiled as I looked around the room at my new colleagues. At least I had the presence of mind not to yawn or rub my eyes as I stood before them. I hadn't actually fallen asleep. I think I would have if she had talked five more minutes before introducing me.

At the morning tea break, I met Malcolm Wright, the Head-of-Fifth-Year. A head-of-year was basically a combination guidance counselor and assistant principal for all of the students in that year (grade). Children started high school at age eleven, so the fifth-year students were fifteen and sixteen years old. Most of them were in their last year of formal schooling. Only a handful planned to attend college. Those who did would stay in high school for another two years, studying for their "A-levels," or college entrance exams. Most of Tilbury's students went right into the work force after leaving school at the end of their fifth year. With the scarcity of jobs in Liverpool, though, many would soon be on the dole. It was little wonder that few had high aspirations or ambitions.

According to Malcolm, I had a fifth year "maths" class that would more than likely give me problems. This class didn't meet at Tilbury High School but at the old Tilbury Boys' School, which was being phased out. Malcolm insisted on driving me the mile or so to the old boys' school. Once there, we walked to my classroom, and he helped me choose the textbook I would use. Although thankful for his help, I was flabbergasted that the choice of texts fell to me. I soon found out why. A complete set of texts was not to be found. Whichever text I chose, I would have to make copies for those students who didn't get books. I was further surprised that the students could not take these books out of the classroom. This limited the homework I could assign. Malcolm had a solution to that dilemma.

"Just put the homework problems on the board," he said. "They'll waste a good ten minutes copying them. Not that they'll actually *do* any of the homework. But they will copy the problems from the board, all the same."

I spent the remainder of the morning getting everything set in my room at the old boys' school. Once the jewel of the local school system, the now crumbling three-story building dated from the late nineteenth century and featured a greenhouse on the roof. My room, on the first floor, was large, with fifteen-foot ceilings and huge windows along the outside wall. The floor was wooden and creaky. With every step I took in the empty room, the reverberation of my hard-soled shoes hitting the floor and the creaking of the old tongue-in-groove flooring combined to produce a very old-fashioned sound. It seemed to evoke a bygone era when teachers wore academic gowns to class, punished recalcitrant students with "the cane," and ruled as veritable masters of all they surveyed in their classrooms. Whether such a time really existed at Tilbury, I don't know. According to a few older staff members, it did, and not all that long ago. I had a feeling that the students I was to meet tomorrow morning, however, would not consider me master of any domain. I hardly knew myself what I was doing or what was expected of me. I would just have to be as prepared as I could and make the best of it. I returned with Malcolm to the main campus.

Jack Dawes, the maths department chairman, gave me the textbooks I would use in my second, third, and fourth-year classes. Most of the books were paperback editions, to be shared among several classes and, like the books at the old boys' school, not to be taken home by the students. Already I was formulating opinions as to why Tilbury was not considered a very good school.

I studied my schedule of classes. Unlike most American high school schedules, it was different every day. The English use a weekly schedule rather than a daily one. The Tilbury timetable contained four seventy-five minute periods each day. I met with my five maths classes two or three times a week, had Wednesday morning and Thursday afternoon "games," or physical education, and was blessed with two preparation periods per week. The school day began at nine o'clock and ended at three forty-five.

81

I also noticed a scheduled gap between the first and second-period classes. This, I discovered, allowed for the teachers' morning tea break. During this time, all the teachers went to the staff room while the eleven hundred students were simply sent outside. The tea, served by the dinner ladies, cost five pence and was served in china (not Styrofoam) cups *with* saucers.

Another civilized aspect of the day was a luxurious hour-and-ten-minute lunch. Today, however, with no students in the building, we had no time limit on lunch at all. I rode with several teachers to a nearby pub, one that many of them frequented during the school year. A few of them would spend their lunch hour there but would not consume any food. On this occasion, I had a ploughman's lunch. It consisted of several kinds of cheeses, bread, and brown pickled relish. It was tasty, although a real ploughman could have eaten two or three such lunches.

With their meals, my friends ordered beer. I was a little taken aback. This would never happen back in Bridgeport. A teacher could lose his job if he came back from lunch with alcohol on his breath! Furthermore, I didn't really feel like a beer, with all the work I had ahead of me that afternoon. So I ordered a cola. Mistake. It came in a rather small glass filled almost to the top. There was no ice. I asked for some. The bartender opened a little cooler, took out a single cube, and carefully floated it on the surface of my cola. He smiled benevolently as though he had done me a great service. Although I thanked him politely, I had to wonder whether the British had some deep-seated aversion to drinking any liquid more than five degrees cooler than the temperature of the room.

We finished lunch and returned to the main campus. I spent the rest of the afternoon in my classroom there. My smallish room was packed with thirty desks. Built sometime in the sixties, it had none of the character of my room at the old boys' school. It was purely functional. I wasted no time daydreaming there. I had to inventory the supplies, get the textbooks ready to distribute, plan how much I would cover, and even do a little tidying.

I couldn't put any names in my grade book because I was given no class lists by the administration. I eventually found out who was in my classes from teachers who had the same classes in other periods and from the students themselves. I was, frankly, appalled by this haphazard organization, although no one else seemed particularly concerned. They just rolled with the punches, or "muddled through," as they said. The English, I was told many times, are experts at muddling through.

I finished getting ready for the opening day of school as best as I could. By the time I left the building, I was virtually alone there, most of the other teachers having long since vanished. I drove back to Thornby Heath and found Susan still working on getting our home in order. We ate dinner, had a leisurely walk around the village, and went to bed a little early. I wanted to be at my best in the morning. Needless to say, I felt more than a little apprehensive. As I would soon learn, I had good reason to be.

5 MW

The next morning, I arrived at school with plenty of time to spare. Not many teachers were there yet. I sat in the staff room going over my lesson plans for the day. I was soon to witness a uniquely English phenomenon: morning attendance.

As the time approached 9:05, the room became busier and busier. It soon resembled the floor of the New York Stock Exchange. An office worker had wheeled in a cart containing every attendance record for every homeroom in the school. As the worker called out names, teachers would shout "here" and rush toward the cart. Other teachers near the cart would see their attendance folders and grab them, sometimes taking friends' folders as well. They would then call out their friends' names and quickly toss the folders over couches, chairs, or tables in the general direction of whoever answered. The heads-of-year joined the fray as well, feeling some obligation to procure the folders of teachers in their year. I was fortunate in being spared a homeroom duty, so I just watched, open-mouthed, as this panoply of yelling, jostling, and arm-waving rose to a crescendo. After several minutes, as teachers scurried to their homerooms, the confusion abated, and a strange quiet settled over the staff room. The office worker with the cart left wearily, and two or three probably unimportant scraps of paper fluttered lazily to the floor.

"Is it like this every day?" I asked a teacher who was seated next to me.

"Like what?" he responded.

"This chaotic!" I retorted. "It seemed a bit disorganized."

"I dunno," he said. "Really didn't notice, mate."

"Well, I'm glad I don't have a homeroom to worry about," I said. "How did you luck out and not get a homeroom?"

"Didn't," he answered, exhaling smoke and crushing his cigarette in a nearby ashtray. "Better go now and take me bloody roll." He smiled, winked, and leisurely walked out of the staff room.

I will admit to being shocked by his attitude at the time. I have since learned that many Brits are just not that concerned about time. Punctuality is not regarded as a virtue. Even the school administration tacitly endorsed tardiness. School was supposed to start at 9:05. The attendance folders didn't arrive in the staff room until 9:04. The "folder auction" took six to eight minutes. It was, therefore, impossible for most teachers to get their folders and make it to their homerooms on time.

At least I didn't have to deal with that. The first period of that day was my preparation period. Second period was my first real class: my fifth years at the old boys' school. The class was called 5MW. The 5 was for fifth year, and the MW for Malcolm Wright, their homeroom teacher. 5MW took virtually all their classes together.

I decided to leave before the tea break to make sure I would get there on time. I had been driven to the boys' school the day before and thought I could make it on my own. I wasn't quite sure, though, so I asked Jim Atwater, the religion teacher, who was the only other person in the staff room.

"Turn left as you pull out of the car park," said Jim. "Turn left at the T-junction, then right at the Nag's Head. The school's on the left. By the way, if you come to the Moby Dick, you've gone too far."

"Thanks," I said. I carefully noted the directions but chuckled inwardly at the same time. In our brief time in England, I had yet to receive a set of directions to any destination that did not include the names of at least two pubs.

I made it to the boys' school with only one wrong turn. I parked in the side car park and walked around to the front of the building. It was tea break here by now, and the boys were packed into the small playground, or yard, in front of the school. Most were playing soccer or just running around on the pavement. A few boys were loitering by the arched Victorian entrance to the school. They were all dressed in dark trousers, light blue or white dress shirts, maroon sweaters, and the maroon, black, and yellow school tie. The clothes were clean but rather worn at the elbows, knees, and cuffs.

"Morning, Sir," they said almost in unison as I passed by them.

"Good morning," I said. "How are you boys?"

They looked at each other and laughed. It had to be my accent.

"We're all right, sir," said one finally. "Are you the American teacher taking Mr. Pierce's place."

"Yes," I replied. "My name is Mr. Meuser."

"Mine's Robert," said the group's leader. "This is Darryl, and this is Nigel. Darryl and Nigel are in your maths class. I have Mr. Wright for maths."

"It's nice to meet all of you," I said. "I'd better get to my room and see that everything is ready."

I went inside and headed for my room. Those students seemed pretty nice. Maybe things wouldn't be as bad as Malcolm thought.

I got to my room and made sure everything was organized. Gradually, students filtered into the room. The bell rang for the start of class. I introduced myself.

"I'm Mr. Meuser," I began. "I'm here on exchange from the U.S. and am taking Mr. Pierce's place this year."

Now in most suburban U.S. high school classrooms, teachers have a honeymoon with their classes that lasts anywhere from one to three weeks. During this period, students are generally well-behaved and interested in starting the school year off right. At the end of the honeymoon, the novelty and freshness have worn off, and students begin to see what they can get away with. I wondered how long the honeymoon would last in this English classroom. I didn't have long to find out, and I didn't need a calendar to measure it. I needed a stopwatch. My honeymoon with 5MW lasted all of thirty seconds.

I had barely begun speaking when the room filled with laughter not unlike that from the group of boys on the steps in front of the school. They were obviously not used to an American accent. I kept talking, and the laughter continued. Eventually it subsided, though, and was replaced by the drone of voices engaged in conversation. They had tuned me out. I felt like a first-year teacher again. In many respects, of course, I was.

"I hope this rudeness is not an indication of how you are going to behave this year," I said with a certain amount of irritation. "If it is, then I can give you lunch detentions since your lunch is right after this class. I had hoped that we could start on a more positive note, though."

For a short time they were quiet. I will have to say that they shamed much more easily than American kids. But their shame was short-lived. The noise soon grew to its previous level. It was time to implement my seating chart.

"Darryl Andrews," I called out as I began the process of seating them. There were several snickers.

"Here, sir," said Darryl. He moved to take his front-row seat.

"Why did everyone laugh when I called your name?" I asked him.

"Because you mispronounced it, sir," said Darryl.

"Well, how do you pronounce it?" I continued.

"Darryl," he said. I barely recognized it. The "r" was trilled, and the "l" was almost swallowed. I knew I could not pronounce it. I didn't even try.

"I'll work on it," I said, continuing with my seating chart. I soon had them all seated alphabetically. I had mispronounced a few names but corrected each one after the snickering told me I'd gotten it wrong. The only name I could not pronounce was Darryl's.

From that point on, I had a name to go with a voice. I put two kids who simply would not stop talking on lunch detention. That seemed to settle the rest of them down a bit. I had planned to tell them about my school in America and answer any of their questions about the United States or about American schools. Their unruliness put those plans on hold. I simply outlined the course and tried to get an idea of what they knew about mathematics. It turned out that most of them knew very little. This class would be a challenge in more ways than one.

The period ended, and they all left, with the exception of my two detainees. I kept them fifteen minutes and then drove back to the main campus to eat a leisurely lunch. Even with my late start, the long lunch hour gave me time to eat, chat with my new colleagues, and even play a short game of cards. My two afternoon classes at the main campus were much better than 5MW. I could see the potential for some really good classes. My problem was going to be that fifth year class.

Over the next several days and weeks, I struggled with 5MW. I kept them busy virtually every minute of the class period. Since there were not enough textbooks, I had to Xerox homework assignments. Once I forgot and was in a small panic until I remembered Malcolm's suggestion to put homework problems on the board for the students to copy. I thought this a terrible waste of time, but I had little choice. After reviewing the homework and discussing the new material, I announced that the assignment would be put on the board. To my amazement, all of the boys immediately got out their notebooks and started copying the assignment. The faster ones were soon finished copying and began working on the problems while the slower ones were still copying when the bell rang. Those still copying continued to do so into their lunch period. They used their own time to finish the copying, though none of them probably had any intention of actually doing the homework. For some reason, they felt compelled to stay and copy every jot and tittle.

This copying, I thought, must be something they had been conditioned to do. I wondered what other activities were part of their conditioning. I decided to find out. Over the next several weeks, I observed as many other teachers as I could. As a result of these observations, I came up with three rules for classroom management that British teachers live by. First, take roll orally. It wastes a good ten minutes and settles everyone down. Second, yell, don't talk. This establishes your authority. Third, whenever possible, humiliate students. They expect it. If you don't do it, they consider you weak.

To be honest, I never followed rules one or three. I just couldn't bring myself to. I did try rule two. Yelling did seem to catch their attention better, but I used it sparingly. It just wasn't me.

One of my observations, by the way, came quite by accident. I was at the boys' school one afternoon supervising the yard during the afternoon tea break. The boys were playing, and I was talking with another teacher on duty. The deputy head, Bertram Fenwick, was in his office. During the course of the break, someone inflated a condom and tossed it into the air. It floated over the yard, bouncing in slow motion a couple of times, while the boys pointed and laughed. I looked at the other teacher, who was himself chuckling. Bertram Fenwick had evidently seen it as well but was not pleased. He came storming out of his office and barked out two words. He sounded like a British drill sergeant.

"Boys! Line!" he yelled. He was angry.

The hundred and fifty boys responded to those two words in a way that astounded me. They instantly scrambled to get to their places in an obviously well-rehearsed line that started at the steps of the school. Twenty seconds later, they were all in a neat queue, standing straight and still, and absolutely silent. Mr. Fenwick walked slowly along the line, looking boys in their eyes as they looked straight ahead.

"Someone thinks that there is something funny about blowing up a condom and floating it over the school yard," he said. The word *condom* stood out, not only because he actually said the word, but because of the way he said it. I almost didn't recognize the word. He pronounced it *cawndawm*, with equal stress on each syllable.

"Well, I don't see anything funny about it at all," he continued. "There's nothing funny about a *cawndawm*. I think we will all just stand here in line for a while and think about how un-funny a *cawndawm* really is."

They stood in line for the rest of the break while Mr. Fenwick continued to upbraid them. The bell signaling the end of break rang, but they waited to be dismissed by Mr. Fenwick. At his word, they walked back into the building, heads bowed.

For my part, I was in awe of Bert's ability to control a hundred and fifty hooligans without so much as breaking a sweat. He obviously had a strong disciplinary reputation. He also, I was to discover as the year progressed, felt deeply committed to the school and to the students themselves. There was almost nothing he wouldn't do for one of his lads, from calling home to check with "mum" about a student's progress to giving a boy lunch money if he knew he hadn't had a meal that day. The boys knew this, and they respected and, I think, loved him for it.

I, of course, had no reputation. It was, at least partially, with this in mind that I agreed to coach the fifth-year soccer team. I thought I might get to know some of the lads better. They didn't really ever practice and had few games, so the time commitment wasn't much. They did seem to appreciate the fact that I had taken an interest in one of their activities, though. In class, I made a point of trying to help each student individually each period. All these little things were slowly making 5MW more bearable. Only one student was still consistently a thorn in my side. That student was Nigel Green.

Nigel was bright. He was also very lazy. He always seemed to understand the mathematics that we did. Perhaps he was bored. His only purpose in class appeared to be to annoy the teacher. And he did this very well. He talked incessantly, for which he served many of my lunch-time detentions. He periodically threw spitwads at the board, although I could never catch him in the act. He questioned almost every assignment that I gave, wondering if he had to do it if he already understood it.

One day, about two months into the school year, the class was working together on an assignment. Nigel had talked

90

through most of the explanation and discussion of the new topic. For once, he didn't know what was going on. He asked to move his desk so he could work with another student. I told him that he must stay where he was because he had not paid attention during the class discussion.

I was called to the door by a knock. It was a student delivering a message from another teacher. I thanked the student and glanced at the note, which was about an upcoming meeting. I turned around to see Nigel sitting next to his friend, having moved his desk several feet to its new location. Most of Nigel's misbehavior was sneaky. This, however, was a direct challenge to my authority.

I had had it. I saw red. I strode over to his desk and quickly and purposefully pushed desk, chair, and Nigel past his old spot and all the way to the back of the room, pinning him against the back wall with the desk. I then made use of rule number two. I yelled.

"When I tell you to work by yourself, that's exactly what I mean. I don't care if you don't like my accent. I don't care if you think you know everything I'm trying to teach you (which you don't). I don't care if you have an excuse for every annoying thing that you do. Right here, right now, and for the rest of the year, you are going to follow my directions to the letter. You are going to do everything exactly as I say. Is that clear?"

"Yes, sir," sputtered Nigel.

The room was deathly quiet. I went back to my desk and tossed my book onto it. It made a loud thud. I sat down and pretended to write something in my grade book. I doubt if I could have really written anything with my hand shaking as it was. But I felt good. If I had strayed over into rule number three a bit, Nigel certainly had asked for it.

My next class with 5MW was two days later. I decided to follow rule number one and take roll orally. I began much as I had on the first day of class two months ago.

"Darryl Andrews," I said, but this time with a perfectly trilled "r" and expertly swallowed "l." I had been practicing.

"Here, sir," Darryl beamed. His grin went from ear to ear.

Also, for the first time that I could remember, I was smiling in 5MW. So was everyone else in the room, even Nigel Green. I continued taking roll, pronouncing all the other names without error. The rest of the class period was productive, almost enjoyable. I felt I had made some sort of breakthrough. We even had that long-postponed discussion about life in the U.S.

There would, inevitably, be more bad days in 5MW. After all, it was their self-appointed task to sharpen the disciplinary skills of their teachers. Happily, the good days would soon outnumber the bad, and the lads in this room would be among those students who gave me the most thoughtful going-away presents and to whom it would be most difficult for me to say good-bye when it came time to leave for good.

Mickey's Bad Day

Mickey Brisbee taught physical education, or "games," at Tilbury. He was between thirty-five and forty years old and very comfortable in his job. Not much upset him, although he was good at feigning displeasure with errant students. He was from Yorkshire and spoke with a decidedly rural accent. Yorkshiremen have the peculiar habit of rarely using the article *the*. Sometimes *the* becomes *t'* or virtually disappears altogether. The statement, "Put the book on the table," would come out, "Put t' book on table." Mickey had lived in Liverpool for many years and, consequently, usually remembered to include a few *the's* in his conversation.

One day, early in the school year, Mickey came into the staff room near the end of the lunch hour. He was beaming. He saw Jim Atwater and me sitting on one of several threadbare and not-too-stylish couches. Jim was the school's religion teacher who, like me, taught physical education on the side. The three of us supervised Thursday afternoon games together. Mickey walked over to us.

"I'm glad I found you both together. I've just had a great coup," he said. In response to our blank stares, he asked, "Isn't that the word I want: *coup*?"

"Depends what you've done," said Jim.

"Well, I'll tell you. I've just had a word with Eleanor Ratcliffe, and she agreed to finish this term with her girls' P.E. classes indoors in the sports complex. That means we get to use the indoor complex next term, just when the worst weather hits in November and December. I don't think she realized what she was doing."

I knew Eleanor pretty well. She and her husband Graham lived in Thornby Heath not far from our house. They had been helpful in getting us settled in and had invited us to a number of activities even in our short time there. Eleanor was a good coordinator and used her skills to run the girls' physical education department as well as various other programs at school. She was efficient in her work and professional yet friendly in her dealings with colleagues. She had her sights set on becoming an administrator. She was everything that Mickey was not. Putting anything over on Eleanor was a rare occurrence.

"That's great," said Jim. "But I thought you had some really important news, lad." He couldn't resist teasing him a bit.

Mickey started to respond but just as suddenly realized that Jim was pulling his leg. With an exasperated wave of his hand, he continued on his way and out the other door of the staff room.

"That is great news," said Jim to me after Mickey had gone. "We'll have a bit of rain this month, but in November and December it rains every day, and it's a cold rain. We'll be thanking Mickey that we're warm and dry inside the sports complex."

The sports complex was part of a nearby community recreation center that the school had use of at certain times of the day. It included a large gymnasium, squash courts, a swimming pool, sand soccer fields, tennis courts, an indoor soccer dome, and an old stadium with an outdoor track. There was not enough room for both boys and girls' classes to use the indoor facilities, so they had to alternate. This was evidently always a bone of contention.

As it was Thursday afternoon, Jim and I decided it was time to walk to the changing rooms under the stadium at the sports complex. The stadium was, in fact, very old and had been used in several scenes in the movie *Chariots of Fire*. Some of the Tilbury students had been extras in the movie, a fact which they related with no small amount of pride.

When we arrived at the changing rooms, we saw Mickey already getting the outdoor equipment ready for the afternoon's activities. Mickey, Jim, and I were in charge of about sixty students that afternoon. Once changed, we proceeded to the stadium itself, where the students were seated.

Like all of his colleagues, Mickey took great pains and quite a bit of class time taking roll. At first glance, this appeared to be a deliberate waste of time. It was that. But it also was a way of easing into a class period. Small tidbits of the students' lives would often emerge.

"Andrews," called Mickey when he was finally ready to begin.

"Here, sir," answered a voice whose body was invisible to me.

Mickey carefully ticked the small rectangle in the attendance record by Andrews' name. He looked up to verify that it was indeed Darryl Andrews who had answered. He knew all the students well since they were the same ones he had taught the year before and the year before that. He also somehow knew exactly where Darryl was seated in the throng of sixty. Having verified Darryl's presence, he cleared his throat in preparation for the next name.

"Braithwaite," he called. There was no response. "Mr. Braithwaite," he intoned, a little louder. There was a quiet chorus of adolescent laughter. James Braithwaite had momentarily dozed off.

"Braithwaite!" yelled Mickey. With a start, Braithwaite lurched forward, hitting the student in the seat ahead of his.

"Uh, here, sir," said Braithwaite, gradually regaining consciousness.

"Working late at the market again, Braithwaite?" Mickey asked.

"Yes, sir. Me mum said I had 'a pay for me own meals now as I'm fifteen.''

"Well, try to stay awake during the soccer game, will you?" concluded Mickey.

"Yes, sir."

The taking of roll went on for another fifteen minutes. There were numerous interruptions: private consultations with Jim Atwater or various students, checking the master schedule when a student was missing, or stopping to chastise students who had gotten into some of the equipment we were to use that afternoon. Finally the roll was completed.

We began our first activity, a "fun run" of five miles through the streets of Tilbury and into a bit of the surrounding countryside. The area was one of the so-called "Green Belts," farmland or forests which surround villages and towns and whose boundaries are strictly enforced by law. It presented a soothing panorama through which to run. My only real duty was to corral the stragglers, so my pace was a relaxing one. I passed two-hundred-year-old farm cottages, ran along wagon ruts that may have been centuries old, and dodged cow patties that were obviously more modern. It was invigorating. All the frustrations I was experiencing in living and trying to teach in a foreign culture melted away.

When I returned to the stadium, I was somewhat concerned that no one was around. Mickey had already broken up the class into groups with designated activities: outdoor soccer, indoor soccer in the dome, and tennis. Most of the boys were already in their assigned locations. I saw Jim Atwater and learned that I was to supervise the outdoor soccer. That I could handle. I arrived at the sand soccer field to find Mickey finishing the selection of the teams. Every English schoolboy can play soccer, and they were all eager to get started.

"Is 'Sir' going to play?" someone asked Mickey. It took me a minute to realize that the "Sir" to whom he referred was I. I knew by this time that British students usually addressed their teachers as "Sir" or "Miss." I had not realized that "Sir" and "Miss" were not only our titles, but also our names, like "Dad" or "Mum." It was not the last time I would be referred to as "Sir" in the third person.

Mickey left me in charge and headed back toward the school. I was glad to have this duty and to play with the boys in a sport that I had coached. I didn't do too badly. They humored me good-naturedly when I would get the ball, knowing that I knew the game but was not an experienced player. There were no uniforms, not even skins and shirts to distinguish the teams. Everyone (except me) knew who was on each team.

After an hour of soccer, I was tired, and fortunately the class was over. I walked back to the stadium and spotted Jim, who had been supervising the lads playing tennis. We headed for the changing rooms where we changed back into our street clothes. As we dressed, Jim expressed some concern as to Mickey's whereabouts. Mickey was always ready to leave at the end of the school day. Jim kept looking around the door to see if he was coming.

A student came into the changing room.

"Mr. Brisbee was in a fight," he said.

"A fight?" we both asked in astonishment.

"Yeah. He and a student were rolling around on the floor in real knock-down-drag-out. It all happened back at the school."

"Was anyone hurt?" Jim asked.

"I don't think so. Mr. Brisbee was pretty mad, though."

The student had to leave. We finished dressing and walked back to the main school building. Immediately upon entering the staff room, we were greeted by Esther Nethercott, the chemistry teacher.

"Did you hear that Mickey was in a bit of a tussle?" she asked.

"Well, yes. What happened?"

"I guess some grotty kid was messing about by the back doors where he wasn't supposed to be. Mickey confronted him, and the kid took a swing at him. One of the shop teachers came and helped him out. They took him to Miss Wimbish. You watch. She won't do anything to him. She's useless."

Before we could respond, the door to the staff room opened. On the other side of the door stood Mickey, seemingly unable to move. He finally shuffled into the room and

97

dropped his obviously weary frame onto the couch next to our small group. There was a silence of anticipation. Finally, Esther spoke.

"For the love of Mike, tell us what happened," she blurted out.

"With what?" asked Mickey.

"The fight, what else?" answered Esther, by now becoming peeved.

"Oh, that. It was nuthun'. Boy was messin' about by back door. I asked 'im where 'e was to be, and t' bugger took a swing at me. Lucky thing it was that Ray Pierson happened along to give me a hand."

Despite his words to the contrary, he was a bit rattled. He was leaving out too many *the's*. Even in a crisis such as this, though, Mickey managed a playful smile. His self-deprecating manner had endeared him to the staff, and everyone was extremely sympathetic. And yet, they all felt that somehow it was Mickey's lot in life always to come up a little short.

As we were to find out, his tale of woe was not over. The fight was the least of Mickey's worries. After he left me in charge of the outdoor soccer group, he had walked back to the school from the sports complex. Of course when he got to the school, he had encountered the student-pugilist. Before all of this, he had sent his group from the games class to the dome to play indoor soccer.

The dome was literally an inflated building. It looked like a blimp that had landed and was partially submerged in the ground. The walls were a soft, rubbery material, and there was no skeletal structure. It was held up by air that was continuously pumped into it. Entry into the building was gained through a double door system. Only one of the doors was to be opened at a time or the air being pumped into the building would escape, and the building would collapse.

This unusual design was a temporary solution to the problem of not having enough indoor recreational space. This "temporary" solution was in its fifteenth year of use and was definitely showing signs of wear. One such sign was a small hole in the side through which some of the forced air would escape.

When Mickey sent his class to the dome, he didn't realize that it was locked. His enterprising students solved that problem by crawling through the small hole to get inside. Unfortunately, this caused the hole to enlarge considerably. After twenty or so students had crawled through it, the once-small hole was now a gaping wound, and the building started to sag noticeably. By the time Mickey had sorted out the incident with the fight at school and headed back to his unsupervised class, most of the supporting air pressure was gone. As he crested the hill leading to the sports complex, his heart sank. Where the dome had once stood, there now rested what appeared to be a giant prune. His class was walking around it, pointing and gesturing.

Before returning to the staff room Mickey had spent an uncomfortable fifteen minutes in the office of the sports complex director. He informed Mickey of the consequences of the afternoon's disastrous events. The boy's physical education classes would not be allowed to use the dome for an undetermined period. Even worse, use by the boys of all indoor sports facilities was curtailed until further notice.

"Me coup with Eleanor has flopped," he said with a forlorn chuckle. Though his shoulders sagged and a great sigh escaped his lungs, there was still the hint of a twinkle in his eye.

"You might as well get used to our English rain," he said to me. "We'll probably be out in it for quite a while."

Queensroad School

Morning tea was such a civilized tradition. From 10:45 to 11:00 every day, the Tilbury teachers would gather in the staff room for a cup of tea and a cookie, served by the ever-faithful dinner ladies. The tea was brewed the English way, not with a dainty individual tea bag per cup, but with loose tea thrown into large teapots and water added just at the boil. To prevent the leaves from entering the cups, the tea was poured through tiny strainers held by the dinner ladies between their thumbs and index fingers. This probably would have been painful had their hands not been made of asbestos.

A noisy affair, the tea break produced a clangorous, happy din. The sound of clattering cups and saucers mingled with the animated conversations of teachers seeking the refuge of fellow adults after having spent the previous hour and a half with uncooperative children. This fifteen-minute safe haven was possible because the eleven hundred Tilbury students were simply sent outside.

One teacher was assigned supervisory duty during this time. The title "supervisor" was a euphemism. That teacher usually stood at the courtyard door where only a handful of students gathered. It took my plodding American brain quite a while to comprehend that the supervisor hadn't the slightest desire to know what the other 1,095 students were doing during the tea break. Not realizing this by the time I took my first turn as supervisor, I made the mistake of actually walking into the courtyard and even onto the grassy playing fields beyond.

As I strolled past groups of students running and playing, I was greeted with stares and open mouths. They must have thought that I was lost. A few of my own students said hello and kindly asked if I needed help. I told them no, thanked them for their concern, and continued breezily on my way, hands in pockets.

I rounded the corner of one of the self-contained mobile classrooms that stood on the grass next to the courtyard and saw a disturbing sight. A girl was lying on the grass just out of sight of the courtyard door while two boys kicked her. She seemed to make no effort to move, and stranger still, no crowd of gawkers had formed to witness the fight, if that's what it was. Although I was unaware of many English customs, I felt sure that this was one not sanctioned by the school. I walked quickly to the little group.

"What's going on here?" I asked.

The boys instantly stopped kicking her and faced me with a look of amazement. They were silent.

"I want to know what's going on here," I repeated.

At length, the girl on the ground spoke up. "We're just toy fighting, sir." She brushed herself off as she got up.

"Toy fighting?" I asked.

"That's right, sir," said one of the boys who had finally found his tongue. "We were just messin' about."

"Well, it didn't look like messing about to me," I countered. "I think we'll just have to pay a visit to Miss Wimbish."

I had been at Tilbury long enough to know that the mere mention of the head teacher's name would not exactly strike fear into their hearts. Miss Wimbish was not much of a disciplinarian. Nevertheless, they didn't really want to go to the office. It took some persuading for them to come with me. By this time, of course, a crowd of students had formed a circle around our little group. As we walked to the office, the circle of onlookers followed us and appeared to grow exponentially. By the time we reached the courtyard, the crowd around us numbered in the hundreds, or so it seemed to me at the time. The miscreants kept telling the other students how unfairly they were being detained. A few in the crowd were starting to turn hostile. The noise level rose several decibels. I was glad we were almost at the courtyard door.

As we arrived at the entrance, amidst all the grumbling and complaining, someone at the edge of the circle of students directly behind us yelled out above the tumult, "Yankee, go home!" Several other took up this chant. I stopped, spun around, and pointed to a boy standing where I thought the catcall had originated. I wasn't totally sure he was the culprit, but at that point I didn't have time to conduct a lengthy investigation.

"You," I shouted, "come with me!"

"I didn't say it," he protested.

"Come with me," I repeated. He reluctantly moved toward us.

Fortunately, at this point, Bertram Fenwick arrived on the scene. Though normally at the old boys' school, he happened to be here at the main campus for an administrative meeting. He had heard all the commotion and came to investigate.

"What's going on here?" he barked out as he exited the courtyard door. At his presence, the crowd instantly dispersed, almost as if on cue. It reminded me of a large production number in a movie musical where highly animated singers and dancers would, at the final chord of a song, suddenly transform themselves into a milling crowd, talking quietly and going about their business, leaving the principal players to carry on with the plot.

Greatly relieved, I delivered the students to him, explaining what had happened.

"Do you allow 'toy fighting' on school grounds?" I asked him before he took the students to the office.

"Certainly not!" he responded, not surprisingly. "We'll get to the bottom of all this, won't we?" he added, looking at the students. Heads bowed, they nodded almost imperceptibly.

Bert saw me later in the day. He didn't tell me how he had disciplined the students, and I didn't ask. I assumed it was appropriate for the offense. What he did want to tell me was that the student I had nabbed as having shouted, "Yankee, go home," was, in fact, the one who did it.

"How did you know who it was with your back to him?" Bert asked me.

"I don't know," I said. "I just turned in the general direction of the yell and guessed."

"Well, the kids think you have eyes in the back of your head," he said with a smile. "Not a bad reputation to have around this place!"

"Thanks," I said, "I need all the help I can get."

Bert started to leave, changed his mind, and took a step back toward me. Though no one else was around, he lowered his voice and whispered conspiratorially, "Most teachers on duty never stray too far from the courtyard door. It *is* easier that way."

"I'll remember that next time," I said. It was my turn to smile.

Even as I became acclimated to the English educational system, I never fully learned what constituted acceptable or unacceptable student behavior. Some things that bothered me, my British colleagues didn't seem to notice, while other infractions, especially small breeches of protocol about which I was completely unaware, sent them into paroxysms of rage. Though it did get easier as the year progressed, I was often frustrated. I spent an inordinate amount of time on matters of discipline and often felt less than completely supported by Miss Wimbish.

I was beginning to think that all English schools were like Tilbury. In accordance with the Fulbright Exchange guidelines, I had been given time off to observe other schools. Most were similar to Tilbury, perhaps a little better organized. I had come to the conclusion that I much preferred Bridgeport to any school I had seen in England. This was before I visited a small patch of heaven on earth called Queensroad School.

At lunch the day after the "toy fighting" incident, Jim Atwater asked me if I had been to Queensroad School. I told him no but that I had one more observation day left. He strongly advised me to see Queensroad. He said I should see how the "other half" lived. Intrigued, I made arrangements to spend a day there during the following week.

On the day of my visit, I left the house earlier than usual. Queensroad was ten miles farther and, I would soon discover, eighty years removed from Tilbury. As I walked across its sprawling, gothic campus, I stepped back in time to about the turn of the century, when the British Empire encompassed a quarter of the earth's surface. This school had provided the empire with many of its leaders, a fact about which it universally prided itself.

As instructed, I found the headmaster's residence. The large, two-story, Victorian home was built with the locally quarried reddish stone that characterized most of Liverpool's architecture. I was greeted at the door by a student assistant and ushered into the headmaster's old-fashioned study. As I walked in, its calm and quiet enveloped me. Wood paneling and bulging book shelves rose to meet its thirteen foot ceilings. Most every horizontal surface teemed with momentos, pictures, and memorabilia. The place conveyed a sense of cluttered tidiness, of disciplined comfort, of polite warmth.

Mr. Rutherford, the headmaster, stepped out from behind the large mahogany desk. He was about sixty-five, tall, gray-haired, and courtly, the quintessential "Mr. Chips." We shook hands and exchanged introductions and greetings. He offered me one of two chairs in front of his desk and sat in the other one himself.

"We are delighted to have you here, Mr. Meuser. We've been so looking forward to your visit."

"Thank you, Mr. Rutherford," I responded. "It's a pleasure to be here. The campus is absolutely beautiful."

I tried to put my best foot forward. Though I could never match his charm and grace, at least I could be sincere. But my plain Midwestern accent made me feel like a flannel shirt at an embassy ball. I needn't have worried. Mr. Rutherford was an expert at putting people at their ease.

"Thank you," he said. "It isn't often that we get to show it off to a teacher from America. It's such an honor to have you here." I almost looked around to see whom he was addressing.

"We'll be pleased to show you several classes," he continued. "Don't expect much in the way of modern technology, though. Sometimes I think we're stuck in the year 1908." He chuckled in a self-deprecating manner. Obviously, though, he was intensely proud of the great traditions of Queensroad and would bitterly fight any untoward twentieth-century incursions into its hallowed halls.

We talked for ten or fifteen minutes, during which time we enjoyed a delightful tea served on china bearing the official Queensroad crest. Although the student assistant brought in the tray, Mr. Rutherford served. As only the English can, he displayed the knack of turning a simple snack into an elegant repast, replete with the time-honored traditions of turning the pot, pouring the tea *over* the milk, and asking that inevitable question, "one lump or two?"

After we finished tea, he told me about my tour of the school. "I'll introduce you to Mr. Southgate, one of our mathematics masters. He'll show you a couple of maths classes and take you to morning assembly. After that, Mrs. Rutherford and I would be pleased if you could join us for lunch. Several instructors will be attending and are anxious to hear your views on education."

"I would be delighted to," I responded. "Thank you."

A knock on the door told him Mr. Southgate had arrived. After the usual introductions, Mr. Southgate and I left him and walked across the garden-like grounds to the mathematics and science building. He wore an academic gown over his tie and suit coat. Several other teachers similarly attired made their way to various buildings. In the blustery wind, their robes billowing, they looked like giant black birds preparing to take to the air.

Before going to class, we stopped by the faculty lounge. In contrast to Tilbury's relaxed atmosphere, this smoke-filled enclave was charged with electricity. Thirty black-gowned men stood, engaged in often vociferous conversation. The room looked more like a judicial chamber than a school

lounge. Mr. Southgate quickly checked his mailbox and introduced me to a few teachers. The bell for the start of class
rang. No one moved. The conversations continued unabated.
After one or two minutes, a deputy headmaster arrived and
verbally and, in some cases, physically had to prod teachers
to get to their classrooms. He was still working on a few as
Mr. Southgate and I left for his first-period geometry class.

When Mr. Southgate entered his classroom, twenty students in dark blue blazers and red and gold striped ties immediately rose and stood at attention beside their desks. His brisk
"Good Morning" was answered in kind by the class. At his
signal, they resumed their seats. After introducing me, he proceeded to discuss the previous night's homework. He encouraged students who answered his questions or asked ones of
their own but verbally brutalized those few boys who were
unprepared. His liberally sprinkled humor was dry and decidedly "insider," which delighted most of his charges.

During the next period, I observed a younger teacher. Mr.
Southgate had warned me that his style of teaching would be
different from his own. It was. He had little control over his
students, who did not rise to greet him, and got almost nothing done. As I sat there, waiting for the period mercifully to
end, I couldn't help thinking that most classes weren't this
bad even at poor old Tilbury. I'm still not sure why they chose
to show me this teacher's class. I guess even paradise can
have its troubles.

Mr. Southgate met me afterward and escorted me to the
assembly hall, where the student body gathered to hear a
guest speaker. Its lobby was decorated with larger-than-life
portraits of admirals, judges, and statesmen, all alums, or "old
boys," of Queensroad. As current students were called
"boys," it was only natural that alumni were known as "old
boys." Most kept in touch with former classmates, providing
business leads or calling in favors, thus forming the "old
boy network."

The assembly speaker was an old boy of a sister institution
in Manchester. He spoke of the many advantages of being
an old boy. Though not from Queensroad, as an alumnus of
an equally prestigious private school, he was still a member

of the "club." This was a club of which I was decidedly not a member. No one at Tilbury was a member, either. By the speech's end, I felt very much an outsider in this world of wealth and privilege. I considered leaving then and there. Were it not for Mr. Rutherford's luncheon invitation, I would have. I'm glad that I didn't.

As I walked from the assembly hall to the headmaster's residence, I felt unsettled at the speaker's attitude of exclusivity and class distinction. Didn't everyone deserve a chance at a good education? Wasn't education supposed to be the great equalizer, enabling anyone to pull himself up by his own boot-straps? Maybe the idea of equality was a uniquely American notion. All of a sudden, the thought of wearing a flannel shirt didn't seem so bad.

I must admit that I went to lunch with a bit of a chip on my shoulder. I was seated next to Mr. Southgate. Four other teachers and the guest speaker sat at Mr. and Mrs. Rutherford's dining room table. Mrs. Rutherford had prepared a sumptuous feast of onion soup, roast pork, Brussels sprouts, and roasted potatoes, with a chocolate torte for dessert. Our wine glasses were never allowed to fall below half full. Mrs. Rutherford did most of the serving. We had again stepped back in time to 1908.

The dinner conversation was stimulating yet non-combative. Most of the diners possessed a rapier wit, which they muzzled somewhat in deference to their host. It would have been bad form to be rude to any guest of Mr. Rutherford, who was, incidentally, the perfect host. He didn't talk that much himself but managed to guide the conversation from person to person and from topic to topic. When he noticed that someone hadn't spoken for a while, he deftly introduced that person's area of expertise into the conversation, thus drawing him into the discussion. Despite my recent feelings of misgivings about Queensroad and its snobbery, I again fell under the spell of his old-world charm.

The conversation drifted to education. The assembly speaker reiterated his position on the advantages of a private education. He didn't call the masses forced to attend public schools a rabble, but he might as well have. He concluded with a question for me.

"Let's hear the American viewpoint," he intoned, turning toward me. "What do you think of Queensroad School? Smashing! Eh what?"

"Queensroad is smashing," I said quietly. "It would be a dream come true to teach here. In the United States, though, we view education as everyone's birthright. Anyone willing to work hard can better himself. From what you have said, it sounds like Queensroad is designed to educate only the privileged few. Is this true?"

Before the speaker could respond, a clarion voice from the other side of the table rang out, "I'd like to answer that." At this, all incidental talking ceased. Those finishing dessert or sipping their coffee stopped and looked up. The voice was Mr. Rutherford's.

"It may seem to you that Queensroad is only for the rich," he began. "Yet, that is not entirely true." As he spoke, he bore no trace of resentment toward my question. He displayed only kindness and patience. He loved Queensroad and wanted his American guest to think well of it. I think he actually felt a little embarrassed by the guest speaker's jingoism.

"While we do depend on funds generated by tuition and endowments, we have a certain amount set aside each year for scholarships. Quite a few of our students have earned merit awards and pay nothing. None of the students or teachers knows who they are, so there is never any social pressure against them. Our main job is to educate all of our students to the highest standards."

"I'm so glad to hear that," I said. "I was beginning to fear that Queensroad's success was precipitated on the mediocrity of the public school system."

"Certainly not," Mr. Rutherford assured me. Others at the table echoed his sentiments.

I made no further comment, and the conversation wound its way to other topics. Secretly, however, I remained unconvinced. As wonderful and caring a headmaster as Mr. Rutherford was, he remained part of a system designed to keep each class of people in its place and ensure the continued dominance of those with wealth and power. Even as I thought this, I was honest enough with myself to admit that had they offered me the chance to finish out the year at Queensroad instead of Tilbury, I would have accepted in an instant.

Back at Tilbury the next morning, I arrived earlier than usual. The old place seemed shabbier than ever. I mentally girded myself for the day's battles and hoped that I would not encounter any more "toy fighting." I made my way through the dingy hallway to my classroom to look over the work my students had completed the day before in my absence. I sat working at my desk when someone knocked on the door.

"Come in," I said.

A shy-looking student cautiously entered the room. He wore a frayed school sweater over a dingy white shirt, a poorly knotted tie, and muddy trousers. I didn't recognize him. He stood by the door, waiting.

"Yes?" I asked.

"I'm sorry," he mumbled quietly.

"Sorry?" I asked again, puzzled.

"Yes, sir. I'm sorry I told you to go home. A bunch o' me friends have you for maths, and they say you're all right. I shouldn't have said what I did. I guess I got carried away."

The light finally dawned. It was the boy who had said "Yankee, go home."

"It's all right," I said. "You were just sticking up for your friends. But you understand I couldn't let a comment like that pass without doing something?"

"I understand, sir," he replied. "What I don't understand is how you knew it was me. You weren't even lookin' at me."

"I have eyes in the back of my head," I deadpanned, not cracking the slightest smile.

For a split second, he stared at me, expressionless. Then a small grin turned into a big one, and finally into a full-fledged laugh. I returned his smile, and he waved good-bye and left.

Nice lad, I thought. I felt sad that he would probably never have the chance to go to college, never experience exhilarating success in the financial world, or ever serve his nation as a great statesman. He was not a member of that club. Neither was I. My place while in England was at Tilbury, where I would try to teach all who came into my classroom, and where I would often measure my own success by the sincerity of a student's apology or the size of his smile.

Independence Day

As the English academic year drew to a close, everyone seemed to move at half-speed. Though the school year ran through mid-July, by the beginning of summer the fifth-year students had begun to take their examinations and were not required to attend classes. Aside from occasionally helping to monitor their exams, I had no more fifth-year duties, either maths or physical education. This gave me quite a bit more free time.

It was fortunate that I had the extra time. Second-year student reports were due. This was a complete surprise to me since Morris Herbert, Head-of-Second-Year, had neglected to mention it to me. He just assumed I knew. Fortunately, I didn't have to calculate any grades. All I had to do was write a short paragraph describing each student's efforts. This report would then be sent home to the parents.

Even without the calculation of grades, these reports required quite a bit of time. I had roughly fifty students in my two second-year classes. It took me several of my new-found free periods to complete them. I ran a day late giving them to Morris, but I didn't care because he hadn't bothered to tell me about them. When I finished the last one, I walked to Morris' room and gave him the stack of reports. He smiled and thanked me but breathed a heavy sigh of relief. He started reading them almost immediately, and I left him to his task. Less than ten minutes later he burst into the staff room, very perplexed.

"You can't say this on a report," he said, holding one of the slips of paper in the air as he approached me. "And these here, they just won't do."

"What's the problem?" I asked somewhat combatively, making little effort to conceal my displeasure with him for springing these reports on me at the last minute and feeling pretty independent, with barely a month left before I would be back in the U.S.

"You said that Claire Boniface didn't pay attention in class," said Morris.

"She didn't," I countered.

"But you can't say that on the report."

"Why not?"

"It's too negative," he tried to explain. "Miss Wimbish just won't allow it."

"Well, it's the truth," I said. "In fact, Claire did almost nothing the entire year. I think her parents need to know that."

"Then say it a different way. Put something positive in the report. Miss Wimbish doesn't want to ruffle any parent's feathers. These other two reports should be revised as well."

"I suppose I could revise them," I admitted. I decided it was simpler just to do it and not cause problems. This whitewash, however, rubbed me the wrong way.

I sat at a table in the staff room and started on the revisions. I had almost finished them when Jack Dawes, mathematics department chairman, came over to me with a stack of papers.

"Here is a test that you need to give to your third years today," he said matter-of-factly.

"Today!" I gasped. "I had planned to finish the review for the mock exam."

"It'll just have to wait," he answered. "All of our third years have to take this test. The results have to be sent in by Monday of next week."

Exasperated, I took the tests, and Jack quickly left the staff room. Louise Milton, the music teacher, came over and sat beside me.

"I couldn't help overhear your conversation with Jack Dawes," she began.

"It's just so frustrating," I said.

"It is a bit late to spring it on you," said Louise, "but think of it this way: you get a free period out of it while the kids take the test."

"Yes, I suppose."

"Why, just yesterday, Malcolm Wright took my fourth-year music class to set up chairs in the hall for a special program that evening," she went on. "I was delighted. I had an unexpected free period."

"In my school back home," I said, "most of my colleagues, myself included, would be furious if an administrator commandeered one of their classes, especially on such short notice. I guess it's just a different attitude."

It *was* a different attitude. Even after almost a year of teaching at Tilbury, I still had not grasped that difference. It wasn't that my English colleagues weren't good teachers. They were. They just didn't consider school and teaching the center of their lives, as American teachers often do. It probably made for a more healthy, though less passionate, approach to the profession.

I took Louise's advice and shrugged off the incidents of poor communication and whitewashing students' reports as learning experiences. I only had a few weeks left and didn't want to leave with a bad taste in my mouth. Besides, the Fourth of July was almost here. I wondered what plans the rest of the staff had for celebrating it. I made the mistake of asking Jim Atwater in front of several other teachers.

"What are you all doing for the Fourth?" I asked.

"What fourth?"

"The Fourth of July. Independence Day, of course."

They all looked at each other. Jim warily eyed me for a moment and then put his hand on my shoulder. "We didn't win that one, lad," he said. "We Brits are a funny lot. We don't normally celebrate the wars we lose."

By this time the others had begun to laugh. I suddenly realized how ludicrous my question had been.

"I guess I wasn't thinking," I replied sheepishly.

"Guess?" said Esther Nethercott. "There's no guessing about it. Your brain was on holiday!" The laughter increased.

"Yeah," said another, "the bloody Fourth of July holiday!"

By now, a chorus of guffaws resounded throughout the staff room. Teachers who hadn't witnessed the original gaffe were filled in and continued the ribbing already underway.

It didn't end there, either. For the remainder of the day and even several days afterward, staff members greeted me with sarcastic comments about getting ready for the Fourth. Some asked about imaginary parades, fireworks, or picnics. One or two suggested that I research other great British defeats and campaign for their national observances. Like some college fraternity pledge, I bore it all with stoic resignation. What else could I do?

By the actual fourth of July, the teasings had subsided. I certainly had no intention of bringing up the subject. If I could just get through the day without anyone remembering that it was America's Independence Day, I thought I would be home free.

My morning classes went smoothly. As usual, I ate lunch in the staff room. Eleanor Ratcliffe saw me at the end of the lunch hour and said that she had a special computer installation at one of the primary schools that she wanted to show me. She thought some connection could be worked up with the computer lab back in Bridgeport. I had no classes that afternoon, so I was more than happy to visit another school.

As it turned out, the visit was less than exciting. Most of the programming pertained to elementary students. We talked about an international computer hook-up in general terms but made no firm commitments. I could hardly do so because I was not part of Bridgeport's computer department.

Eleanor, who had left midway through the visit, reappeared in time to take me back to Tilbury before the end of the school day. She took a wrong turn, though, and we arrived at the school a good ten minutes after the final bell had rung. The hallways were virtually deserted. I had left my briefcase in the staff room, so Eleanor and I walked there to pick it up.

As I opened the door, I was greeted by seventy-five voices yelling, "Surprise!" It was the entire staff of Tilbury High School. They had secretly planned an Independence Day party for Susan and me. The computer trip to the primary school was a complete ruse, it being necessary to get me out of the building to prepare for the party. Eleanor had left the primary school to drive to Thornby Heath and pick up Susan, who was in on the surprise. She had driven so fast during all of this that she actually made it back to the primary school too early. She solved that problem by conveniently taking a "wrong turn."

The party was smashing. The staff room was decorated with balloons, crepe paper, and over one hundred American flags drawn and colored by the Tilbury special education students. It must have taken them days. A few of the flags sported blue stars drawn on a white background, but that was the fault of their teacher!

More amazingly, every staff member wore a costume, portraying some sort of American character. Esther Nethercott dressed as Sue Ellen Ewing from *Dallas*, one of England's favorite American television programs. Mickey Brisbee wore a basketball player's uniform. The fact that he was only five feet seven inches tall only increased its comic effect. One teacher, a bearded man of about two hundred and fifty pounds, was dressed as Shirley Temple. Southern belles, wild Indians, and a few Presidents were among the partiers. Jim Atwater, dressed as a *M.A.S.H.* character, served as master of ceremonies.

"Ladies and gentlemen, or should I say guys and gals," he began in a charming but poorly affected American accent, "because Mark and Susan don't have anyone in the whole of England to help them commemorate this day of American Independence, we have decided to do just that. Before we begin, however, we should point out to Mark that the British don't celebrate the Fourth of July." Roars of laughter greeted this last comment. I had to laugh myself, and as I looked into the faces of my colleagues, I saw their broadly smiling eyes returning my gaze and knew that this time they were laughing *with* me. Perhaps they always had been.

"Accordingly, since the British don't observe the Fourth, today we are all Americans," stated Jim. A few in the crowd responded with a decidedly British-sounding "hear, hear." The rest applauded.

"Just look at our fancy dress!" he continued. "Did you ever see a more American group? Now let's get down and party!"

We ate hamburgers, hot dogs, and potato crisps, and drank beer, wine, and champagne. Eleanor Ratcliffe organized a lively square dance, accompanied by an old recording of English folk music. After the dance, I made my way around the room, greeting everybody and commenting on each of their unique costumes. The abundance of alcohol seemed to enliven the festivities. I told several of them that if U.S. teachers brought alcohol onto the school grounds, they would be promptly and unceremoniously fired. They couldn't understand that, shaking their heads in disbelief.

I chatted with Jack Dawes, who had dressed as a cowboy. He gave me a hearty slap on the back and said what a pleasure it had been to work with me. Morris Herbert was a football player. He spoke in glowing terms of my teaching and of my contribution to the school. I was glad that I never actually verbalized my resentment toward either of them over the unannounced testing or whitewashing of student reports. I felt small for even having thought unkindly about them.

The party continued for well over an hour. Five of the women teachers dressed as cheerleaders and performed cheers that they had written themselves. These cheers poked fun at a few of Tilbury's "finest," cast aspersions at educational big-wigs, and creatively mentioned some of my own escapades during the year. The staff applauded and cheered each one a little louder than the last.

Sylvia Pymer, a physical education teacher, then took center stage and did an impersonation of Miss Wimbish disciplining a recalcitrant student, portrayed by Eleanor, who had changed into a Tilbury uniform. Eleanor perfectly lampooned a gum-chewing, teenage ne'er-do-well, while Sylvia had Miss Wimbish down to a tee, complete with glasses, which she put on and took off almost continuously. The staff didn't even try to contain their amusement over this parody of an administrator of whom they were not overly fond.

Finally, Miss Wimbish, who had not deigned to dress in costume, presented me with several gifts and mementos of my stay there, including a large picture book of England and a photo album of pictures of Tilbury. I, in turn, got out of my locker the American flag, which I had brought from my U.S. classroom, and presented it to the school. Miss Wimbish received it graciously and promised to hang it in a place of honor in her office. This statement was met with audible groans from the staff. The flag never did make it to her office but hung in the staff room, at least until I left.

The party wound down, but I was reluctant to leave. It was one of the good times, and I wanted it to last. This outpouring of warmth and camaraderie from the staff would make it all the more difficult for us to say our final good-byes a few short weeks later. That party cemented a bond of friendship that time and an ocean couldn't break.

I still keep in touch with several of them, especially at Christmas. Some have since retired or left teaching. Sadly, one or two have passed away. But the friendship, spirit, and loyalty of that British faculty remains fresh in my memory, in part, due to what might be the only celebration of America's independence to take place on British soil. After that day, the Fourth of July has never been the same, and neither have I.

IV. Administrators: Don't They Get It?
The Grade Change

For some reason, the enclosed, air-conditioned walkway designed to connect the cabin of the plane to the interior of the terminal was not functioning. We had to use an old-style stairway to the simmering pavement and walk about a hundred feet to the terminal. Stepping out of the plane into the August heat and humidity was like stepping into a furnace. At that moment I felt more British than American. I had forgotten how hot it could get in the Midwest and regretted every joke I had made about the cool, rainy English weather.

For the last month or so of our year in Britain, I had longed to get back to Bridgeport. I wanted to see friends and family and to settle back into our house and get ready for the new school year. Now that we were back, though, I found myself thinking more and more about the good times we had enjoyed in England. I missed not only our English friends but also the culture itself. Feeling in a way like a "citizen of the world," I wasn't ready to resume our old life.

Like it or not, I didn't have much time for such musings. The list of chores loomed large. The day after we got back, I drove to school and stopped by the main office. I wanted to see my class schedule and pick up a few classroom supplies. The only one in the office at the time was Dan Williams, the principal.

Dan was the administrator I had angered early in my career when he was still an assistant principal. As the years passed, he rose through the ranks of administrators and became high school principal about three years before we went to England. He had done a creditable job at the helm, and we had a cordial relationship, if not an overtly friendly one. Still, I was somewhat surprised when he greeted me warmly and insisted on taking me on a tour of a newly-renovated section of the school.

The renovated building was the oldest one on the high school campus, dating from the 1920s. Though still used for classes, its crumbling walls, peeling paint, leaking roofs and windows, and antiquated plumbing and heating systems had needed major renovation. As luck would have it, the entire job was completed while we lived in England.

Classrooms were enlarged and updated, hallways were remodeled and brightened, and the old auditorium was replaced with a beautiful fitness center. It was really impressive. Dan was obviously pleased with the results. Phrases like "state of the art" and "best in the county" punctuated his commentary as he showed me the building. Walking through the beautiful renovation, however, I kept wondering why I was getting such VIP treatment. Was Dan expecting some payback later? Or was he just being friendly and trying to start our year on a positive note? I really didn't know.

The new school year began well. Teaching in the renovated building was a pleasure. My only complaint was that the old floor tiles had been covered over with carpeting so I couldn't use my infamous grid system for keeping the desks in their proper locations. After teaching a year in a foreign country, though, it was reassuring to return to an American classroom, where I knew what textbooks I would be using, what behavior to expect from the students, and the level of cooperation I could count on from the administration. My classes were excellent. They enjoyed hearing stories about my year in England, and not just because that meant we had temporarily strayed off the mathematical topic of the day. They seemed fascinated by first-hand accounts of life in another culture.

For my part, I was determined not to get locked into old habits. If teaching in England had taught me anything, it had taught me flexibility. I felt that I could now roll with just about any punch that was thrown my way.

That punch was several months in coming.

One of my algebra students that year was a girl named Grace Peterson. Being partially deaf, she had a special tutor from the learning disabilities department of our school. Grace was a very quiet girl in class but was always pleasant and hard-working. About half way through the year, however, something changed. Her efforts lagged. Homework assignments were not done. Her test grades plummeted. I talked to her about it, and she promised to do better, but she continued on her downward spiral. She eventually failed the third quarter by one point.

I was not surprised to get a call from Grace's mother. She had not responded to the mid-term progress report that I had sent home. Perhaps she thought that Grace's work would improve. The cold, hard "F" on her daughter's report card was inescapable evidence that it hadn't. She was now very concerned.

"She was only one point from passing?" she asked at one point in our conversation.

"Yes," I answered. "She had a 64 percent."

Mrs. Peterson was a polished and well-educated woman. What she said next, I felt, she said with great difficulty.

"Would you consider giving her that point?" she asked. Her words spoken slowly, as though they were painstakingly formulated.

My own response was equally painstaking.

"I don't really feel that I can do that," I said.

"Would you think about it?" she asked, this time much more quickly.

"I will re-calculate her grade and make sure it was truly a 64 percent," I answered, "but if that is her grade, then it will have to stand."

"I see," she said. "I'll look forward to hearing from you."

I said good-bye and hung up the phone. I knew I had not made a mistake on her grade, but I dutifully recalculated it. There was no change. I called Mrs. Peterson the next morning and told her. She thanked me and concluded the conversation.

My own attitude toward giving students points was one that had developed over many years. It was, more or less, the same view held by almost every other teacher I knew. Giving points to pass a student who actually didn't was a dangerous precedent. It undermined the integrity of the grading system, lowered standards of achievement, and cheapened the efforts of those who legitimately passed. Occasionally, I might have a student who had worked tremendously hard but still failed. If that student's grade was within a point or two of passing, I always gave him the benefit of the doubt. If a student had not done homework, taken few notes, and shown little interest in the class, however, the grade would have to stand on its own merits, or lack thereof. Grace had placed herself squarely in this latter category.

By the end of the day, a note was in my mailbox asking me to stop by the principal's office before I left school.

"I understand that Grace Peterson failed algebra by one point," Dan Williams said matter-of-factly as I sat down across from his desk.

"Yes," I said warily, not knowing what he was up to. A tiny warning bell went off somewhere in the back of my mind.

"Did you know that she is a pretty good sprinter for the track team?" he asked.

"I had heard that."

"Well, if she doesn't pass algebra, she'll be ineligible to participate," said Dan.

"What's your point?" I responded. "She has already failed."

"Not if you change her grade to a 'D,'" he said.

"What?" I asked. I knew I had heard him correctly. I still found it hard to believe that those words had come out of his mouth.

"If you pass her, she'll be able to run track," he continued, not even noticing the shock registered on my face or in my

121

voice. "Especially since she's deaf, it will be good for her to be on the team. You really ought to pass her."

"Dan," I began slowly, pausing to choose my words carefully, "Grace failed because she didn't do her homework and didn't study for tests. She didn't try. It would be wrong to pass her when she didn't deserve to just so she could run track."

"I disagree," he said. "Sometimes you just have to bend the rules."

I didn't say anything.

"Well, you think about it," he finally concluded.

"There is nothing to think about," I said. "I am not changing that grade."

By this time, I didn't feel any need to maintain even the pretense of cooperation over this issue. What he had suggested ran counter to everything I believed in. Yes, while in England, I had revised those second-year reports for Morris Herbert. There, however, I was a guest, and I felt obligated to follow their guidelines for writing reports. This was my country, my school, and my own integrity. I wasn't about to do something I felt was very wrong.

Dan made a noise like he was going to say something but didn't. I left his office without the usual exchange of departing pleasantries.

Even though I had told Dan that I had nothing to think about, over the next several days I thought of little else. I worried that I was being too harsh on Grace. Maybe I should give her a break because of her handicap. I had never had to struggle with deafness. Perhaps I would view the situation differently if I had. I decided to call my cousin Jane. She had worked for many years as a teacher at the state school for the deaf. I explained the situation to her.

"Did she fail because she was deaf or because she didn't work?" Jane asked.

"I would have to say because she didn't work," I replied. "There were several homework assignments that she didn't even bother to turn in."

"Then you owe it to her to let her grade stand as an 'F,'" she said. It was an interesting way of phrasing it. She went on to explain. "If you give her a grade she doesn't deserve, you are telling her that she doesn't have to be as good as everyone else. You would be allowing her to use her handicap as an excuse when it really isn't. She's not mentally handicapped, is she?"

Jane's last question had cut to the heart of the issue. No, Grace was most certainly not mentally handicapped. She was very bright. She had just stopped working. From that moment on, I had no more doubts about what I should do. I simply could not change that grade.

Early the next week, I was informed of a meeting called to discuss Grace's algebra grade. I didn't understand why anyone other than Grace or her teacher should determine her grade. Still, I had no choice but to attend the meeting. In attendance were Dan Williams, who chaired the meeting, Bob Gerald, an assistant principal, and Diana Carver, head of special education services. She herself had tutored Grace on occasion. We met in a conference room adjacent to the guidance office.

"I've asked everyone here," Dan began, "to help determine what should be done about Grace Peterson's algebra grade."

I didn't say anything. I felt like saying he was out of line in calling such a meeting, but I didn't, perhaps because I also felt like a fly in the presence of three spiders.

Dan asked Diana to speak first. She outlined Grace's progress over the past year and basically asked me to be lenient in considering her grade. She was handicapped, after all. She did mention that Grace had also failed English, but by ten or fifteen points. This was, I felt, a tactical error on her part.

"Why did she fail English?" I asked her after she had finished.

"I think it was because she didn't turn in some book report," she said.

"That's exactly why she failed math," I responded. "She didn't turn in several math assignments, any one of which would have boosted her grade to a passing mark. I would like to know if her English teacher is being asked to pass her as well."

"No," answered Dan.

"Why not?" I asked.

"Well," he began slowly, "fifteen points is just too far away from passing." He tilted his head and grimaced, as though he truly wished he could change her English grade, too.

"What's the difference between changing that grade and changing her math grade?" I asked.

"Fourteen points," quipped Bob Gerald. I'm sure he said that to break the tension which was, slowly but surely, starting to build. It was a pretty funny rejoinder, too, but no one laughed. I was too upset, and the other two were simply caught off guard.

Bob was a former teacher and a good friend. He honestly cared about students. His position on this issue, however, was diametrically opposed to mine.

"Have you ever been in a situation," he said, looking directly at me, "where you came up a little short and somebody gave you a break?"

"I suppose," I said cautiously. I could see where he was headed. Diane had argued for sympathy. Bob opted to work the guilt angle. He did a pretty good job of it, too.

"I thought so. And you've never had a handicap to deal with. Can you imagine what that would be like?" he continued. "All we're asking here is that you give her a break!"

For the next twenty minutes, all three of them kept hitting those two themes: sympathy and guilt. Dan was becoming exasperated that I still had not changed my mind. He was also getting angry.

"The girl's handicapped, for crying out loud!" he boomed. "Have you no compassion?"

"That's it," I said. I was mad, too. There was no point in holding anything back. "I'm sure the three of you think that I don't care about Grace and that I haven't even considered changing her grade. That is not true. I have thought about it ever since the issue came up.

"I even called my cousin who taught at the state deaf school for many years. I asked her what she would do. Do you know what she told me? She said under no circumstances should I change that grade. She said it would send Grace a very bad message: that she, as a partially deaf person, is not as good as everyone else because she doesn't have to meet the same

124

standard as everyone else. You cannot change her grade without imparting to her second-class status. And I will not do that. Grace needs to know that she is accountable for the decisions she makes."

Dan started to say something.

"Let me finish, please," I quickly interjected. "No one has mentioned the real reason we are here. After all, this grade of 'F' is not her final grade. It's only her quarter term grade. She has plenty of time to raise it. Even if she doesn't bring it up, she has enough credit from the first semester to pass the course for the year. No, the real reason we are here is athletics. Grace can't run track because she hasn't passed enough courses this grading period. I will not be a party to changing a grade for athletic convenience. I think it's wrong. The athletic tail will not wag this academic dog!"

"You're wrong about athletics being the real issue," said Dan. He had cooled down considerably. "It is a sidelight, that is true. Doing the right thing for Grace is the real issue. We would be here whether Grace was in athletics or not."

The meeting was soon adjourned. Everyone had expressed his opinion. Nothing was resolved. Two more such meetings took place in the same number of days, one with Dan and Bob, and the other with Dan alone. The results were essentially the same. Dan did tell me when we met alone that he was considering changing the grade without my consent. I told him that if he did that, I would file a grievance against him through the education association.

As luck would have it, a meeting of the high school members of the education association was held later that week. After dealing with some preliminary business, the chairperson asked if there were any concerns. I briefly, and without specific names or details, outlined my recent troubles. Quite a bit of discussion followed. For my own curiosity, I asked how many others had been pressured to change a grade by the principal. Of the fifty people there, thirty hands went up. The scope of this problem was larger than I had imagined.

For all its potential to develop into a first-rate donnybrook, the Grace Peterson incident ended ignominiously. I received word that her grade would not be changed. It seems that

Grace had been caught smoking in the girls' restroom. A three-day suspension from school and automatic removal from any athletic team were the standard punishments. Even Dan Williams couldn't get her out of it. Under the circumstances, Mrs. Peterson didn't wish to pursue the change of her daughter's math grade.

Later in the day, I was walking past Dan's office. He asked me to step in and have a seat. He explained what had happened to Grace. I told him I had already heard.

"I just want you to know," he said, "that I would have changed her grade if she hadn't been caught smoking."

I didn't remind him of his denial that athletics was the main issue. Neither did I reiterate my position of filing a grievance if the grade were changed, although I would have. I figured I would just keep him guessing as to my intentions. I merely thanked him for informing me of the most recent developments and then left.

I thought back to my year teaching in England. Recalling the second-year reports that I reluctantly revised, I realized that over there I wouldn't have made this kind of fuss over anything. And although I wistfully envisioned that relative lack of responsibility, I was, nevertheless, glad to be back in a place where I cared enough to take a stand. I guess that's the difference between being a visitor and being at home. As great a year as I had experienced in England, I knew I belonged here.

Cheaters Never Prosper?

Eric Pugh was a likable kid. He was captain of the boys' volleyball team and popular not only with athletes but also with most other students at school. He wasn't quite as popular with his teachers. There were two reasons for this. He didn't do much in the way of schoolwork, just enough to get by. He also insisted on being the center of attention in most of his classes, and not through his academic contributions.

I had Eric for second-year algebra. I think he enjoyed the class fairly well. He maintained a respectable "C" average and kept his classroom antics to a minimum. As long as he didn't overdo it, his classroom comedy injected some personality into the class. I was able to play off his humor and make the lessons fun. Having one or two funny people in a class made developing a rapport with that class much easier. I think Eric somehow understood this. I couldn't help but like him.

Eric usually knew where the line between acceptable and unacceptable was drawn. He might edge up to it and dance around it a bit, but he wouldn't knowingly cross it. At least I didn't think he would. I found out differently after a particularly difficult test in the second grading period.

At the end of the day that we took the test, I received a note from Catherine Gray. Catherine was an English teacher who was nearing retirement age. She had a reputation for being tough but fair. Her note said that Eric had, during their study time, circulated around her classroom loudly asking for the questions on his upcoming algebra test. The test was the next period, and he was hopeful that someone from my morning class would give him the questions ahead of time. Even though the questions were usually different, knowing them ahead of time would give a tremendous, unfair advantage. Catherine might never have noticed him had it not been for his propensity to call attention to himself, even while doing something he wasn't supposed to. She concluded her note to me by stating that she was sure I would want to know what he had done.

I'm not sure I "wanted" to know. I needed to know, though. What he did was a form of cheating. He would have to receive a zero for that test, according to school policy.

The next day, I saw Eric before class so I could talk with him privately before I passed back their graded tests.

"I have a note here from Mrs. Gray," I began. "It says that you were asking people in her class about the questions on our algebra test during the period before this class."

Eric was silent.

"Well, were you?" I asked.

He was still silent. This time I decided to wait him out. I didn't say anything either. Eric finally spoke.

"Man, everybody does it," he complained. "It's no big deal. I don't know why you're picking on me."

"I don't know about anybody else. I do know about you," I said. "You tried to get the questions ahead of time, didn't you."

"I guess," said Eric. It took several second for him to pronounce the last word. The final "s" was punctuated by a sharp exhaling of breath. He had conceded my point, but he wanted to show me that he was not pleased.

"Eric," I said, softening a bit, "I know people try to get answers before tests. That's why I make two different tests.

But your trying to get those answers in front of Mrs. Gray was not the most brilliant of moves."

He chuckled in spite of himself. He wasn't entirely ready to give up, though.

"What business was it of Mrs. Gray's anyway?" he asked. "She's just a busybody."

"She's not a busybody. She's just doing her job. You know, it seems to me that you need to stop blaming everybody else and just admit that you made a mistake."

"The only mistake I made was getting caught," he said.

At least he was honest. I suppose a large percentage of the population would agree with him. I didn't.

"Getting caught wasn't your mistake," I said. "It was merely the consequence of your mistake. Your mistake, Eric, was cheating."

I didn't really think that I would change his mind. I had to try, though. Eric was uncharacteristically quiet for that whole period. I knew it would take a couple days for him to return to his usual self. Although I usually appreciated his classroom humor, I decided to enjoy his self-imposed silence while it lasted.

The following day I got a call from Mrs. Pugh. She was not pleased that Eric had gotten a zero on the test.

"He didn't really cheat," she said, "and other kids did the same thing and didn't get a zero."

"He tried to find out the test questions before he took the test," I answered. "That's cheating. And he did it right in front of a teacher! If there were other students doing the same thing in private, there is no way I can punish them. Eric did this publicly. I found out about it, and now I have to deal with it."

"He only tried to find out the questions, not the answers. He figured those out for himself. It's not cheating if you don't ask for the answers."

I honestly couldn't believe she said that. Over the years, I had heard many parents deny that their kids would ever cheat. I had heard some give excuses for their kids' cheating. Yet I had never heard a parent actually defend cheating. I felt like asking her if she knew the difference between right and wrong. But I didn't. I was polite.

"Mrs. Pugh," I said, "the question here is whether Eric tried to gain unfair advantage over the other students by finding out about the test beforehand. The answer is 'yes, he did.'"

"Well, I think you're being too harsh on him. He's a good boy," she said, pausing. "I just hope he's not going to be ineligible for volleyball because of this."

I could see where her priorities lay. "I don't know about that," I responded. "I'm more concerned that he will able to put this incident behind him and do well in the course for the rest of the year."

"Well, yes," she admitted. "I'm still not happy with the way you're handling it. I may see the principal about this."

I was not pleased that she was going to drag out this issue, although I had to admire her forthrightness in telling me her intentions. Many parents would have said nothing and gone to the principal behind my back.

I told her that was fine and that she was within her rights to take it up with an administrator. We said good-bye.

Karl Strawser was the building principal at the time. He was one of a succession of principals after Dan Williams. He was hired because he had a reputation for a no-nonsense approach to running a school. Such an approach was deemed necessary because in recent years, discipline in the hallways and around the school had been in decline. Citing the need to treat each situation individually, well-meaning principals were loathe to enforce school rules consistently. As a result, many teachers retreated to the safety of their own classrooms and stopped disciplining students in the halls. They didn't know whether the administration would support them or not. Pushing, shoving, swearing, and even fighting became commonplace. Academics and learning suffered. Though many tried, no one seemed able to remedy the situation. Then came Karl Strawser.

Karl was a mild-mannered, soft-spoken man. He appeared to follow Benjamin Franklin's axiom of never expressing an opinion too vehemently on either side of any issue. This appeared at first to be timidity or even weakness. It was, in reality, a manifestation of tremendous strength and self-confidence. He had no need to prove anything to anybody. Karl had two rules. First, he did what he felt was right, not politically expedient. As a result, plenty of chips had fallen where they might. Second, everybody had to follow the rules. He made virtually no exceptions.

He had little patience with students who hindered the learning of others. He exercised consistent discipline, suspended troublemakers, and supported his teachers. The enforcement of one rule, in particular, set the tone for the school. That was the "no hat" rule. If a student wore a hat in the building, he lost it. No warning, no argument, no hat.

While some civil libertarians might decry the deprivation of this chapeauic liberty, our staff flourished under it. In just one year, the hallways became as pleasant as they were in the "good old days." Students' respect for teachers and for each other increased dramatically. Tensions in the halls eased. Academics enjoyed a resurgence.

So it was that when Mrs. Pugh said she was taking the cheating issue up with Mr. Strawser, I felt confident in the outcome. The day after my conversation with Mrs. Pugh, Karl asked me into his office.

"Mrs. Pugh called yesterday," he said. "I told her I would speak with you about the cheating incident involving Eric. I also told her that she shouldn't hold out much hope that the grade would be changed, as I trusted your judgment in the situation."

I was pleasantly shocked. Most administrators I have dealt with would have listened sympathetically to the parent and promised to get back with them. Their responses would be veritable studies in non-commitment. Karl was different. He spoke his mind.

"I appreciate your confidence in me," I said. I went on to explain the situation briefly. Karl slowly nodded his head after I had finished and paused for several seconds.

"I don't see how you could have handled it any differently. It's a clear-cut case of cheating," he concluded. "I'll call Mrs. Pugh."

I left the office feeling that all was right with the world. I didn't even have to persuade him that Eric had cheated. He obviously had his own well-established view of academic misconduct. I had never dealt with an administrator of this caliber. There wasn't any feckless hand-wringing either. Eric cheated. That was it.

Unfortunately, that wasn't it. Mrs. Pugh was not satisfied with Karl's ruling. She appealed Eric's case to the superintendent of schools.

Superintendent Curtis was fairly new to the district. He had his doctorate in education and had served as an assistant superintendent in several school systems. This was his first fullfledged superintendancy. He seemed friendly and caring and was well versed on the latest educational research. He had one disconcerting characteristic, however. He could speak at length about almost any topic without actually saying anything. He was highly skilled at it. Though many tried, none could pin him down on any issue of substance.

At the beginning of his tenure, he and Karl saw eye to eye on most issues. As time passed, however, it soon became apparent that they looked at things from completely different perspectives. Karl called a spade a spade. Dr. Curtis might talk about a gardening-based soil relocation implement but would be loath to give it an actual name.

Dr. Curtis heard the Pugh appeal in the conference room of the district's central offices. Of course, Mrs. Pugh and Eric were there. Karl Strawser and I were also there. In his introductory remarks, Dr. Curtis never used the word "cheating." I felt slightly uneasy about that.

"We need to determine if Eric assimilated test-related information in way that is inconsistent with our stated goals and philosophies as set forth in school district policy," he said. "Let's hear from both sides of this issue."

Both Mrs. Pugh and Karl Strawser expressed their views on what had taken place. I added specific details and explained why I gave Eric a zero on the test. For his part, Eric only answered questions that were put to him, usually monosyllabically. He was obviously uncomfortable.

The facts of the case were not really in dispute, only their interpretation. Mrs. Pugh stated that many other students had asked their friends about the test questions. They were not being punished. Punishing only Eric was unfair.

Karl and I pointed out that Eric had certainly tried to gain unfair advantage over other students. Whether other students had cheated or not, Eric was the one who was caught. The fact that unknown, unnamed students may have done the same thing didn't erase what Eric had done or condone it.

After considerable discussion, each side was starting to say the same things and make the same points. Dr. Curtis decided that the meeting had gone on long enough. He thanked everyone and stated that he had a solution that he was sure would satisfy all concerned.

"It appears that Eric did try to gain an advantage," he began. "Even so, I don't think that he thought there was anything wrong with what he did. Accordingly, we will throw out the test that may be 'tainted,' and Eric will be given a chance to take a different test. That way, the results will be valid."

I'm sure Dr. Curtis felt that his solution was one worthy of Solomon. He obviously wanted to please everybody. I, for one, though, was not pleased. I was stunned. This decision set a dangerous precedent. The validity of one test grade was not the point. The school's attitude toward academic misconduct was. Dr. Curtis had just sanctioned cheating.

Karl Strawser was also stunned. He quietly rose from his seat and left the meeting room without a word. I looked for him in his office back at school. He had already gone home.

I did see Karl the next day. He had cooled down some but was still in shock. We were both appalled by Dr. Curtis' decision but agreed that there was nothing to do but chalk this one up to experience. Eric passed his make-up test with a "D," which was lower than his ill-gotten grade of "B," but higher than the zero he should have had. He graduated at the end of that school year and went off to college the following autumn. I often wondered whether he ever learned to stand on his own feet, without cheating on tests or depending on his mother to fight his battles. I know he didn't believe the old axiom, "cheaters never prosper." Yet I hoped that he might eventually realize that he paid a very high long-term price for his short-term prosperity.

That spring, Karl Strawser got an offer to go to a large, prestigious high school in the Boston area. He took some time to decide but eventually accepted the new position. I wondered, but never asked him, if the lack of support from the superintendent figured into his decision to leave. Whether it did or not, we lost one of our very best administrators.

Of course, we still had Dr. Curtis.

PPO's

Teachers usually view themselves as being in charge of their own classrooms. While this is true to a certain extent, they are, like any employee, responsible to their superiors. They must answer to the building principal, the superintendent, the board of education, and ultimately to the voters and parents in the school district. They are influenced by two other groups, as well: the state legislators, who often determine what shall be taught, and the state department of education, which determines how it will be taught and who is qualified to teach it.

State legislators should, I feel, be forgiven for passing laws that are detrimental to education. After all, they are not trained as educators. No one expects them to know anything about how students learn or what is involved in educating them. Further, being politicians, they have to be concerned more with how things look than with how things actually are. That's their job.

The state department of education, on the other hand, is a group of professional educators. They should know better than to mandate unproven systems and unrealistic requirements. Many of them have not been in charge of a classroom for years. Otherwise, they would never propose half of what they do. One particular travesty instituted by the state department was boldly touted as the cure-all for every mathematical ill imaginable. It was known by its major feature: "Pupil Performance Objectives," or PPO's.

I first heard of PPO's at a math curriculum-writing meeting. Assembled in the conference room of our district's central offices were teachers from every school in the district. Fred Finley, math department chair, and I represented the high school. I had been to several such meetings over the years and expected to hear the same old instructions on writing curriculum. I was surprised, then, when George Finch, our Assistant Superintendent for Curriculum, opened the meeting by announcing a veritable revolution in curriculum requirements. This revolution would wipe out mathematical ignorance, he said. This revolution was called "Pupil Performance Objectives."

"In five or six years, we won't even offer courses like general math," he beamed. "Our students won't need it. They'll all be ready to take algebra and geometry."

"How will this happen?" asked Fred. The tone of his voice and his raised eyebrows conveyed more than a hint of doubt. He had heard fantastic claims from various educational gurus during his many years of teaching. Few had been anything more than a flash in the pan.

"I'll explain," answered George, undaunted by Fred's skepticism. "We'll break each level of math down into its basic skill components. Each teacher will have to record each student's proficiency for each skill. The students will have to demonstrate skill mastery three out of four times."

"It sounds like a lot of record-keeping," said Fred.

"Whose idea is this?" I asked. George was quite competent as curriculum superintendent, but he was not one to devise a scheme with such far-reaching consequences.

"It comes from the State Department of Education," he answered. "We are one of the first schools to pilot the PPO program."

"Does this mean we have no choice in the matter?" I asked him.

"I don't want you to think of it in those terms."

"Do we have a choice?" I asked him point-blank.

"No," he said. "I guarantee you, though, that by the end of our meeting, you will be convinced that PPO's are the way to go."

We worked all morning. The elementary teachers were busily writing literally hundreds of PPO's. They devised plans to measure everything from adding two digit numbers to recognizing geometrical figures. Mastery of a skill was defined as three successes out of four attempts. Fred and I, on the other hand, were baffled. We couldn't figure out how to turn the complicated reasoning processes of high school algebra, geometry, trigonometry, and calculus into single-skill check-off lists. We worked on the curriculum guide but included no PPO's. Even George couldn't help us. I think he was starting to have doubts about PPO's himself.

"We'll get some people from the state department in here," he said. "They'll help us write the PPO's for the high school math courses."

"And if they can't," Fred interjected, "we need to write something that sounds great and satisfies their requirements. Then we file it away in some drawer and never look at it again."

"We can't do that," George chided him.

"Why not?" asked Fred.

"I'd lose my job," said George.

"Your job," Fred pointed out, "is to shield your teachers from all the garbage that the state tries to force on us. This whole scheme will do only one thing: make more work for teachers. Good teachers know what their students understand and what they don't. No PPO checklist will take the place of that."

"What if the state department comes out to check on us?" asked George.

"Then we pull the PPO's out of the drawer and show them how wonderful they are," Fred answered.

"At least let's see what the state department people have to say," added George.

Both Fred and I agreed to that.

So it was that two representatives of the state department of education were invited to our next meeting. Catherine Walton and Dell Tucker joined us in the conference room two weeks after our initial meeting. They were both state department employees and former teachers. I suspect they had been out of the classroom for quite some time. Miss Walton was somewhere between thirty-five and forty. She was well-dressed but wore no make-up. With her slightly graying hair pulled back in a bun, she reminded me of many of my own elementary teachers: serious, almost austere. She was quite comfortable taking charge but didn't seem to relish the task. Her colleague Dell Tucker, on the other hand, looked like a successful businessman. His suit was impeccably tailored. He radiated confidence in the brief informal gathering before our meeting, slapping the men on their backs and warmly shaking the women's hands with both of his. I couldn't decide whether Miss Walton, who did most of the talking, was his superior or whether he was hers and simply allowed her to answer most of the questions.

George Finch started the meeting with a warm introduction of our guests. They seemed delighted to be here. They spent quite some time explaining PPO's.

"If we can categorize their math skills and concentrate on the ones they're deficient in," said Miss Walton, "then we'll wipe out math illiteracy in five years."

"Isn't that what good teachers do already?" asked Fred.

"I'm sure they do, but this will just systematize the process," said Miss Walton.

"It sounds like a tremendous amount of paperwork to me," I ventured. "What's wrong with the current system of grades to determine a student's progress?"

Miss Walton inclined her head slightly. A magnanimously knowing smile crept over her face. She briefly explained the theory to us again as though we were a little slow.

"You see," she concluded, "the key word is intervention. You'll teach each student what he doesn't know."

"How do you write a PPO for a course like Geometry?" I asked. "How can you categorize geometrical proofs using single-skill PPO's?"

"Just list the skill you want the student to know," she explained. "The success rate should be three out of four times."

"What about a proof like the Pythagorean Theorem?" I pressed her. "Do we want them to be able to prove it three out of four times? I don't think so. Memorizing proofs is not what geometry is all about. We want them to be able to apply the Pythagorean to other proofs, problems, or situations."

"Then just write down what you want them to know and include the success ratio that you expect," she said.

"Give us an example," said Fred.

"You just take the skill you want them to ...," she began.

"Give us a specific example!" Fred interrupted. He was starting to get angry and had turned beet red. Fred knew when he was getting the run-around. "Give a specific geometrical PPO," he repeated slowly and deliberately. He looked at her directly. His pencil was noticeably poised to copy the words he was waiting to hear.

No words came. Miss Walton was temporarily speechless, her austere countenance frozen in a hesitant intake of breath. I frankly don't think she had the foggiest idea how to write a geometrical PPO. I doubt whether such a task was even possible. The silence was long enough to be slightly embarrassing. Dell Tucker felt obligated to join the fray.

"Perhaps if you would give us a specific topic," said Dell, "we could help you out." Dell's manner was calm and reassuring. Whether he was Miss Walton's boss or underling, his tone told us that he was stepping in to rescue her.

"We gave you a topic," said Fred. "The Pythagorean Theorem."

"That is so broad, though," said Dell. "Can you narrow the scope so as to increase our short-term specificity?"

I cringed. He was starting to talk in "educationese." This was a sure sign that he, too, despite his self-assurance, didn't have a clue as to how to write a geometrical PPO.

"All right," I joined in, "give us a PPO for using the Pythagorean Theorem to find the sides of an isosceles right triangle. Is that specific enough?"

"Yes," said Dell. "What you would need to do is identify and categorize the basic cognitive skills that go into the process, and then determine the success percentage that would constitute skill mastery."

"You do that!" said Fred. "Just tell us what the damn PPO would say!"

This time Dell was silent. He was holding his hands up and looking at the ceiling. He nodded his head a couple of times but still said nothing. He hadn't lasted even as long as Miss Walton. I seriously doubted that he was her superior.

"Each district would have to determine that for itself," said a seemingly recovered Miss Walton.

"How?" I asked.

"By carefully outlining the skills necessary to complete a task."

"Please tell us exactly how to do that," I said. For a third time, there was a long embarrassing silence.

Fred leaned back in his chair, looked at George, and pointed the paper on which he was taking notes at a nearby filing cabinet drawer. I know George got the message.

"I'm sure we'll be able to work these problems out," said George, mercifully rescuing Dell and Miss Walton. "Thank you so much for seeing us today. We'll have to get to work now, and we certainly don't want to take any more of your valuable time."

George saw them out, chatting amiably, while the rest of us on the committee pretended to get back to work. We were actually comparing notes on their complete failure to explain PPO's. Even the elementary teachers on the committee were suddenly much less than enthusiastic about embarking on a time-consuming scheme that even its creators hadn't completely thought out.

We spent the remainder of the day working on the curriculum document. As they were almost done with their PPO's anyway, the elementary teachers wrote a few more and called it quits. Fred and I simply converted our old curriculum to PPO language so it would conform to the standards set forth by the state guidelines. We had absolutely no intention of using any of it.

"You know," said Fred to George as we worked on the re-write, "this whole curriculum guide is headed for the drawer."

"I know," said George. "I caught your signal during the meeting. I can't actually condone burying it in a drawer, but I don't blame you after the state department's debacle today."

"At least one positive result came out of today's meeting," said Fred. "If they can't even tell us what they want, they can hardly reject anything we send them."

"You're probably right about that."

After one more meeting, the curriculum document was finished, proofed, and typed by secretaries in the central office. It was sent on to the state department and, as Fred had predicted, received almost perfunctory approval.

The elementary teachers of our district were thus faced with a mountain of new paperwork, categorizing and recording students' math skills. High school teachers used the curriculum guide as we always had: to make sure we taught the required material. We ignored the PPO's.

Despite the fact that the elementary teachers were using the new PPO's, their students coming to the high school in the years immediately following its inception did no better or worse than students of prior years. Elementary teachers complained about the unnecessary paperwork.

The next curriculum rewrite mandated by the state came about six years later. No mention was made of PPO's. The "PPO Revolution," which was to wipe out math illiteracy, was a thing of the past.

Instead, however, came a new buzzword: "strands." Strands were recurring themes that appeared in many different mathematical topics. The whole curriculum was to be reorganized and cross-referenced according to these strands. This curriculum re-write would probably take twice as long as the last one.

George Finch had left the district a couple of years earlier. The new curriculum superintendent was young and eager to produce a splendid curriculum document. Fred and I again represented the high school. Our goal was far less ambitious. We just wanted to get the thing done with the minimum amount of damage caused by the state department's ivory-tower mandates.

We assembled in the conference room of the newly remodeled central office building. Teachers representing every school in the district were again in attendance. No one knew exactly what to expect from the new assistant superintendent.

"We have a unique opportunity to write a curriculum guide that will raise our students' mathematical understanding to an unprecedented level," he began. "It will be a long and difficult process, with no guarantee that it will be accepted by the state department. Does anyone have any suggestions for the group as we begin this process?"

Fred raised his hand. He had a twinkle in his eye and a wry smile on his face.

"I think we need help on this one from the state department," he said. "See if you can get Catherine Walton and Dell Tucker to come out and explain the new requirements."

The assistant superintendent thought that was a good idea and promised to contact them. Although he tried several times to set up such a meeting, he couldn't get either one of them to come to Bridgeport. For some reason, they were never available. It was thus without their expertise, ultimately, that we labored over yet another document that was destined for the filing cabinet drawer.

V. Teachers Are Human, Too
Moon Over Toledo

Ever since that first educational conference where I heard Birdie Langley speak, I resolved to keep up with new ideas and developments in the teaching of mathematics. I kept hoping to hear a speaker as inspiring as Miss Langley. Over the years, I saw many outstanding presentations, most informative and many extremely entertaining. None, though, ever quite matched her speech from long ago.

I had spoken at one or two conferences myself. One year I was scheduled to speak about my experiences teaching in England through the Fulbright Teacher Exchange Program. I had slides, a running commentary, and samples of English educational materials. I was excited to get the chance to tell my story.

Fred Finley, longtime math department chairman, was to accompany me, as he had many times in the past. Together, we had visited such exotic locales as Cleveland, Fort Wayne, and Indianapolis.

Fred was a unique teacher and personality. He had dual certification in mathematics and English. He was an expert on the Civil War, having read every available book on the subject. A veteran teacher, he had taught every math course in the curriculum with a combination of humor and nonchalance that made him very popular with his students. He was a brilliant analyzer of human behavior and a tough negotiator in curriculum meetings. He was also socially stuck in the seventh grade!

"Hey. Come here!" he would half whisper and half yell, motioning me over to where he was standing in front of his classroom door. Thinking it was something important, I would walk over.

"What do ya know?" he asked.

"Fred! You made me walk all the way over to your room to ask, 'What do ya know?'?"

"Uh, no. I wanted to ask you something," he said.

"OK. What is it?" I asked, although I knew fairly well what was coming.

"Why was the bicycle lying on the ground?"

"Fred!"

"Because it was two-tired. Get it?" he asked. By this time he was laughing uncontrollably, head tilted back, mouth open. For a while, he was the only one laughing. Only rookie teachers laughed at Fred's jokes. Gradually, though, I started to laugh in spite of myself. Students in the hall who hadn't even heard the joke started to laugh. Fred slapped a couple of them on the back as they entered his room. He was still laughing. He finally started to cough. The laughter abated then died away completely. There followed two or three contented sighs, from both of us.

"Don't take any wooden nickels," he said.

"I'll see you at lunch," I responded.

When I told other colleagues that Fred and I were traveling to a math convention together, I could tell that they either pitied me or thought I was crazy for voluntarily spending two days in close quarters with Fred Finley, let alone having to sit through meetings where they talked about "math." Actually, I looked forward to these annual events. They all began the same way: Fred and I in a car on our way to some far-flung outpost of mathematics education. We always had a rather serious discussion about problems at school, the state of education in general, and how things were in the "old days."

Fred's sense of direction was non-existent, so I usually drove. This year, however, Fred had purchased a new van and volunteered to drive. I would, of course, navigate. The conference was in Toledo. Most of the trip was an easy drive through prosperous countryside. We passed ancient barns with old German names painted on them. The accompanying farmhouses were often brick and built in the imposing federal style. Neighboring towns were Victorian showplaces, sometimes restored, sometimes crumbling. It was a journey through history.

As we neared Toledo, the pace of traffic picked up. The conference was in a downtown hotel, and because of his unfamiliarity with the city and its increasingly congested streets, Fred was a nervous wreck by the time we got there. We checked into the hotel and put our luggage in our room. I immediately headed for the conference. Fred headed for the snack bar.

After the morning sessions, we met for lunch. My own presentation was scheduled immediately afterward. I got to the room early and set up the slide projector, screen, and my modest English textbook display, and taped a map of England to the board. Quite a few people started to come into the room. I was pleasantly surprised that the room was soon filled to capacity. Seated in the audience was Dr. Schiller, my old college advisor. He had retired long ago but remained active in mathematics circles. He made a point of attending any conference where a former student was speaking.

The talk went well. Quite a few teachers were interested in doing an exchange themselves, and I gave them information and addresses. The presentation attracted more than a few dyed-in-the-wool Anglophiles. I tried not to burst their bubbles about dear old England, but I was candid in my representation of modern life there.

When I spoke with Dr. Schiller after the session, he mentioned that he'd been to England many times, often with groups of students. He seemed to know every town, village, and county and spoke knowledgeably about their educational

145

system. He never said it in so many words, but he radiated a sense of pride in my successful exchange. He expressed interest in even the smallest details of my experience.

I was delighted that everyone seemed to enjoy my presentation. Even Fred made it through the session without falling asleep. Afterward, he decided to visit the book displays while I attended one more meeting. By four o'clock, though, we were both ready for a break, so we decided to explore downtown Toledo.

The hotel was adjacent to a refurbished riverside shopping area called Portside. We checked out the stores, bought a lottery ticket, got something to take back to our wives, and decided to walk a little more before we ate dinner. Fred didn't want to venture out in his automobile unless it was absolutely necessary.

We found a Spaghetti Warehouse restaurant several blocks away. It was, true to its name, located in an old warehouse. We waited in the basement bar area before we were seated to eat dinner.

"You know, Mark, our Board of Education is getting a real deal with us on this conference," Fred remarked as we waited.

"How so?" I asked. Fred's attendance at one forty-five-minute session was hardly my idea of a "real deal" for the Board.

"Those administrators in the district go off to Las Vegas or Florida, and the Board pays for everything: air fare, meals, conference fees," he said.

"They pay our expenses, too," I ventured.

"But we drove. And to Toledo. Toledo, Ohio! And here we sit ready to eat spaghetti when we should be having steak at some fancy restaurant."

"Well, maybe you're right. Let's have breakfast in the hotel dining room in the morning instead of trying to look for a cheap coffee shop," I said.

"Now you're talking!"

We were soon seated, and the conversation drifted to other matters. We had a nice, relatively inexpensive meal and started to walk back to the hotel. It was early spring, and we were heading into a cold wind whipping in from the north.

146

"We ought to call a cab and charge it to the Board," Fred said, shivering just a little.

"Maybe there is a place we could stop in and have a nightcap—on the Board, of course," I said.

As we walked along, we realized that nothing else was open. Downtown Toledo at that hour was not exactly bustling. We passed a run-down building that at least was lit. It turned out to be a bar with a live show entitled "Adam and Eve." Upon reflection, we decided not to go in. Fred thought that the Board would probably not have picked up the tab.

Once back in our hotel room, we decided to visit the health club in the lower level of the hotel. We put on our swim trunks, grabbed a couple of towels, and took the elevator to the basement. The health club was open but absolutely deserted. Not even an attendant was on duty. After a few pedals on the stationary bicycles and a try at their weight machines, we thankfully eased into the whirlpool. It was wonderful. We must have sat and talked for at least half an hour. Then Fred rather abruptly decided that he was done. He got out of the whirlpool and headed toward the shower. Obviously thinking that this was a men-only section, he started to take off his trunks on the way to the shower.

"Fred! This is a coed area," I warned him. "Someone could walk in from the hall any second."

By this time his swim trunks were down around his ankles, and he was in a panic. He tried simultaneously to run to the shower and pull them up. This was not possible. By trying to pull up his trunks, he prevented himself from taking full strides. He was seemingly running, but with steps so tiny that he appeared not to be moving at all. And because his legs were moving, those trunks were never going to make it up to his waist. His ample frame was thus bent over double, hands around ankles, and hobbling vainly toward the shower area.

He finally made it to the privacy of the shower. A few minutes later he emerged, swim trunks firmly positioned around his middle. We looked at each other and burst out laughing. We laughed about it on the elevator ride to our room, and again at breakfast the next morning. In fact, with Fred's permission, I told the story in our math office the next Monday morning, much to the delight of all in attendance. In the years since the Toledo trip, I have told the story countless times, often to people who have heard it before.

Yes, the Board of Education got its money's worth when they sent Fred and me to Toledo that year.

Reindeer Roundup

In the days before "politically correct" meant anything more than reporting to the right precinct on voting day, the male members of the teaching staff of Bridgeport High School had a long-standing tradition. One evening after school during the week before Christmas vacation, we would assemble at a bar or night club sufficiently far from Bridgeport so as not to be observed by any Bridgeport locals, and celebrate the upcoming holiday. The festivities would start around 7:00 P.M. and wind down by about 10:00 or 11:00, as we would all have to get up for school the next morning. This yearly ritual came to be known affectionately as "Reindeer Roundup."

Despite its name, it was usually a rather calm affair. It was a chance for teachers to get together with friends, complain about problem students to decidedly sympathetic ears, and generally solve all the problems of the world. As soon as the date was set, calendars were cleared of any extraneous activities, and everyone eagerly awaited its arrival. Some teachers even scheduled tests in their classes the following day so that they wouldn't actually have to teach so soon after the roundup.

Reindeer Roundup's last year was by far its most memorable. In fact, it was its notoriety that led to its demise. It began much the same as it always had. We had chosen to meet at a new night club in the *Europa*.

The *Europa* was a relatively new shopping area on the north side of the city. It was built to look like a European village. A central gathering area, known as the "Commons," housed fast-food restaurants serving international cuisine and a number of small gift and import shops. From there one could saunter along stone-paved pedestrian walkways lined with stores of every sort. They were all done in pink and white stucco with stone archways and small-paned windows. Exclusive apartments on the second and third floors of these stores added to the European flavor. The crowning touch was a piazza with a flower-encircled fountain and a statue of a World War I soldier.

Not far from the fountain, down one of the walkways was the Lazy "S" Saloon. That name, of course, did not exactly exude European charm and grace. The Lazy "S" made no pretense toward sophistication. It was a Country and Western bar. The large neon sign on its roof had the "S" conspicuously tilted to reinforce the notion that it was actually lazy. The bar featured live country music and was packed to the rafters almost every night of the week.

I arrived at the Lazy "S" a little after seven o'clock. I found our group at a couple of tables in a corner by the jukebox. I was startled but pleasantly surprised to see Rud McGrath seated at one of the tables. Rud taught math, and although he was no newcomer to the faculty, this was his first appearance at a Reindeer Roundup.

"This is a pretty tame party," he said to me as I sat down. "What can we do to get things rolling?"

"I don't know," I responded. "I heard they had a Bluegrass band that's pretty good. Maybe that will liven things up."

"I sure hope so. I'm getting bored just sitting here talking."

My attention was diverted to Frank Kershner, a history teacher, who was telling a story about a retired colleague.

"So Old Tom was sitting in his classroom the last period of the day," Frank related, "when all of a sudden, three big fire engines roared past the school. He instantly turned on his police scanner, which never left his side, and found out where the fire was.

"Well, Old Tom told his students to keep working on their assignment. He calmly stepped out of his classroom, walked down the hall and out the door. He got into his car and took off like a bat out o' hell after those fire trucks. The only reason I knew that he left was that one of his students eventually knocked on my door and said that Mr. Kennebrew had gone. The class had finished the assignment, and they wondered what they were supposed to do. I told them that Mr. Kennebrew would probably be back momentarily. The student said that he didn't think so because they had seen Mr. Kennebrew leave in his car."

"How did he get away with that?" asked another teacher at the table.

"Well, Old Tom was teaching in the annex at the time, and no administrators ever went over there. Plus, the rest of us in the annex covered for him once we realized what had happened. Old Tom only had two months 'till he retired, and we didn't want to see him get fired."

"If it had been any of the rest of us, the administration would have found out, and that would be the end of our career," said Rud. We all agreed. Old Tom, we marveled, was surely a lucky son-of-a-gun.

About this time, Fred Finley, math department chairman, and Jesse Pratt, school custodian, arrived, and the whole story had to be re-told for their benefits. The story seemed to grow with the re-telling. Perhaps it was the effect of an additional drink or two, but the final version, I think, had Old Tom actually riding one of the fire engines as it sped away from the school.

There followed many other stories, most of them about school. Several teachers shared their best and worst jokes, all of which got funnier as the evening progressed. Eventually, the Bluegrass band started to warm up. When they began to play, several couples from all over the club migrated to the dance floor. The first number was a lively tune, the kind that required at least a foot to be tapping along. The teachers, who now filled three tables, added to the general air of merriment with enthusiastic but miss-timed hand clapping and periodic shouts of "yee-hah." Fred Finley and Jesse Pratt were so caught up in the excitement that they decided to get up and dance themselves.

Fred and Jesse were both large men. Neither was much of a dancer. Had their wives been with them, they wouldn't have dreamed of stepping out onto the dance floor. But they danced to that Bluegrass tune in what could only be described as a cross between "The Twist" and a highland jig. They didn't actually touch one another. Occasionally, one would bump the other with his ample stomach or backside and send him reeling. It was a sight to behold. All the teachers left their places at the tables and formed a circle around them, cheering them on. Frank Kershner began to play the jukebox as though it were a piano. The other dancers even stopped to watch. It was like a scene from a Fred Astaire and Ginger Rogers movie, where everyone in the ballroom had stepped back to marvel at the dancing couple in the center of the floor. By the end of the song, most of the other patrons of the bar were watching, clapping, and cheering our two dancers. Everyone seemed to be having a good time.

The management of the bar evidently wasn't. As the applause died down, one of the bartenders approached Fred and Jesse.

"You two can't dance together," he said curtly.

"Why, what's the problem?" asked Jesse.

"We don't allow people of the same sex to dance together," he said. He was polite, but there was more than a trace of disgust in his down-home voice.

"But you don't think ...," Jesse began.

"Just get off the dance floor," the bartender interrupted. This time he wasn't polite.

Fred and Jesse returned to their seats, not wanting to cause trouble. The mood at our tables turned from jovial to quietly tense. After all, teachers are not used to being on the receiving end of a stern lecture. Gradually, though, with a few well-told stories and jokes, some of the lightheartedness returned to the group. We were soon all laughing as we had before. All of us, that is, except Rud McGrath.

Rud was the type of person whom you tried not to anger. As a student at Bridgeport, he had been something of a troublemaker. He had graduated, earned his degree, and returned to his alma mater to teach and coach. As a former problem student, he knew all the tricks of the trade and put up with none of the shenanigans that he had perpetrated as a student. Rud had the knack, no matter how original any student's misbehavior, of making him feel as though it had been done a hundred times before.

"You tried the old 'spitwad on the end of a pencil' routine?" he would ask a freshly-nabbed suspect, laughing all the while. "That's older than I am and never worked very well anyway."

Students didn't cross Rud. Neither did teachers. I suppose bartenders should be added to that list as well.

Rud didn't say much after Fred and Jesse were banished from the dance floor. I knew he was not pleased, though, with what had just happened to his two friends. He had been trying without success to open a bottle of ketchup for a sandwich and fries he had ordered. As Fred and Jesse sat down, Rud took the bottle in his mouth and bit the cap off. A few shards of glass fell to the table, but he didn't seem to notice. He had consumed quite a bit of alcohol and was settling into a state of quiet, single-minded anger. He was mad at the Lazy "S" Saloon and all who were associated with it for embarrassing his friends.

As Rud ate his meal, the band continued to play. After several numbers, their vocalist got up to sing. She wasn't very good. Her voice was only slightly less grating than fingernails scratched across a blackboard. Still, it wasn't really her singing that aroused Rud's wrath. I think it was simply the fact that she was the most visible representative of the bar at that moment. As such, she became a lightening rod for Rud's simmering hostility.

"You stink," he yelled.

She ignored him.

"No, you really stink," he persisted. "Yes, I'm talking to you," he said, jabbing the air with his index finger. She couldn't ignore that.

153

"C'mon buddy, give me a break," she said, trying to be diplomatic.

"You don't deserve one."

"Why, you're nothing but a male chauvinist pig," she finally cried.

The band was vamping while she jousted with Rud. By this time, though, the rest of us had succeeded in quieting Rud. The same bartender had started toward our tables, but as we indicated that everything was now under control, he turned around and went back to the bar. We asked Rud if he would stay quiet, and he nodded. I thought the worst was over. I was mistaken.

The band decided to take a break. As luck would have it, the only empty table in the bar was right next to Rud's. Band members carried their drinks over to this table and started to sit down. The vocalist was the last to arrive. She started to sit down. Rud was sitting close enough to nudge her chair slightly with his foot so that when she sat down she was barely on its edge. She lost her balance, spilling some of her drink, and nearly falling to the floor. The chair did fall over.

She was furious. The rest of the band was ready to fight. The other teachers were horrified at what was happening but powerless to stop the unfolding chain of events. Rud, at the center of the melee, sat smugly finishing his own drink. Perhaps it was the menacing nonchalance with which he sipped his beer and eyed the angry musicians that kept them from actually going after him.

At any rate, it was time to leave. We tried to get Rud to get up and go. Several bartenders were heading in our direction. One of them went over to Rud and asked his name. With great dignity and deliberation, Rud rose to his full height and loudly proclaimed, "I, sir, am Dr. Charles Carruthers, superintendent of Hampton Heights City Schools." Hampton Heights was a very affluent community not far from the Lazy "S." Its school system had a national reputation, and its superintendent was a leader in the state's educational community.

"Come on, Chuck," I said, playing along. "We've got to get you home."

We bundled him out, got in our cars, and made our get-aways with the sound of approaching police sirens ringing in our ears. I was never so glad to get home in all my life.

Although the evening's festivities had concluded unexpectedly early, morning came all too soon. I arrived at school and went through my usual routine. Everyone who had been at the Lazy "S" the night before, including Rud, reported to his first-period teaching assignment in shirt and tie, bushy-tailed if not bright-eyed.

It was about noon that panic began to spread through the faculty. Our own superintendent was on the rampage. It seems he got an angry call from Dr. Carruthers of Hampton Heights City Schools accusing some Bridgeport teacher of impersonating him in a bar and acting in a way which would defame his character and reputation. Our superintendent had promised to get to the bottom of it. There was talk of a lawsuit.

Nothing ever came of it. I don't know whether the identity of the culprit truly remained a secret, or whether our superintendent just decided to keep a lid on it. In any event, word was sent down that there would be no more Reindeer Roundups.

Thus came to an end a tradition of a bygone era, and later Christmases came and went without so much as a reindeer's hoofbeat on the dance floor of the Lazy "S" Saloon.

VI. Teaching Kids: More Than Teaching Math
This Isn't Ozzie and Harriet

It all started with a dare.

My third period algebra class a few years back didn't believe I had the courage to attend a rock concert. I told them that they didn't have the open-mindedness to attend a symphony orchestra concert. Thus challenged, we neither had any choice but to rise to meet it.

Third period was one of those special classes. I liked to tell classes in subsequent years that this third period was my best reciting class. We memorized theorems and mathematical rules in rhymes and jingles. All of my classes did this because I made them. But third period truly loved it. Every word was spoken in unison. Every line was phrased with precision. They got to a point where they all laughed together, sighed together, and even, I believe, thought together. They were a class in sync, both with each other and with me.

If it had been any other class, I would have laughed off their challenge, and it would have been forgotten the next day. Third period, though, didn't forget. They kept asking me when I was going to attend a rock concert. I finally told them I would go if they made all the necessary arrangements. The class agreed to chip in to buy not only my ticket, but also a pair of blue jeans and a concert T-shirt. I didn't have either, and they said that I couldn't go without them. If I wore my usual shirt and tie, they added, I would probably be killed.

Three members of the class—Bill Laufer, Kevin Gault, and David Wilson—took it upon themselves to buy the tickets. They would also accompany me to the concert. It wasn't so much that they wanted me to go with them, although they thought that would be kind of fun. What they really wanted was to see their favorite rock star. This performer was so well known that he usually went only by his first name, which they told me. Though I had heard of him, I feigned ignorance.

"I didn't think Ozzie Nelson was still alive," I said to the entire class, giving a subtle wink to a couple of students in the front row. "And besides, he wouldn't be doing rock concerts anyway."

"It's not Ozzie Nelson!" screamed several students who had missed the wink. They couldn't believe anyone could be that out-of-touch with the current music scene. A few of them had dropped their heads and were simply shaking them back and forth.

"It's just Ozzy," said Kevin after the class quieted down a bit. "His full name is Ozzy Osbourne."

"He's great," said David. "He bites heads off bats. It's so cool."

"It sounds disgusting," I replied. "Has the man been checked for rabies?"

"He doesn't do that anymore," said Kevin. "He kind of got in trouble with the police over that one. It was on the news. Didn't you see it?"

"I must have missed it," I conceded.

"Well, you're going to love his concert. He puts on one of the best light shows you'll ever see." Everyone agreed.

I wasn't so sure. Besides symphony concerts that Susan and I had frequented, the last popular music concert I had attended was when I was in college. The sixties vocal group The Lettermen had visited our campus and given a concert.

It was wonderful. We packed the college gymnasium to the rafters. In those days, everyone dressed up for concerts. The guys all wore coats and ties, and the girls wore dresses. Even the performers wore ties.

I suspected that both the dress and the atmosphere of the upcoming Ozzy concert would be markedly different. I was not mistaken.

As the day of the concert neared, we made our final preparations. I bought a pair of jeans, for which third period took up the promised donation. From this money they would also purchase my concert T-shirt. Kevin provided me with an Ozzy shirt to wear, as I wouldn't be able to buy one until we were actually there. Another third-period student, John Braun, loaned me his leather jacket. It was spring and still chilly at night, so I needed to stay warm. My tan and corduroy car coat, however, would simply not do.

I took one precaution that I kept secret from third period. Don Townly, the chemistry teacher, was an expert skeet shooter. He had heard that I was attending a rock concert and made a point of giving me a set of earplugs. He said that they would muffle rifle shots and even artillery but made no promises about rock concerts. I thanked him and tucked them into my pocket. As it turned out, they were a godsend.

On the day of the concert, third-period kids were beside themselves with anticipation. They could hardly concentrate on algebra. Their usually precise recitations were almost nonexistent. All they could think about was the concert.

"You have to tell us all about it!" said one girl who had never voluntarily said anything in class before. I promised that I would.

The concert was in Dayton, which was about an hour and a half drive from Bridgeport. Kevin, Bill, David, and I left in plenty of time, almost right after school. I drove. We stopped for dinner along the way.

We arrived so early that the arena where the concert was to take place wasn't even open yet. We wandered around for a while. Walking toward the rear of the building, we noticed a large number of concert groupies milling around service entrances and loading docks hoping to catch a glimpse of

Ozzy or even speak to him as he entered the arena. They all had long hair, multiple tattoos, and appeared to be not totally aware of their surroundings. One giant of a man with a long sandy-colored beard sat on the roof of his car, beer in hand, shouting genial obscenities at friends similarly perched on a car about fifty feet away. He wore torn and faded jeans and a small tank top, which was unsuccessful in covering his large midsection and whose straps cut two narrow paths through gelatinous, hair-covered shoulders. His car apparently doubled as a makeshift home, with pillow, bed sheets, and empty fast food cartons vying for space inside. Old newspapers were taped to the rear window, barely affording him a modicum of privacy. My student charges wanted to stop and gawk, but I hurried them along.

By the time we had circumnavigated the arena a couple of times, the line to get into the concert had started to form. We took our places and waited about twenty minutes before it began to move. During this time, a security guard walked the length of the line shouting that everyone would be checked for weapons before being allowed in. My three students were in line just ahead of me and buzzed with excitement at this announcement. They thought it would be "so cool" to be checked for guns and knives. The guy behind us had a different reaction. He turned to his girlfriend with a panicked look on his face and asked her if she would take his stiletto, as they would be less likely to find it on her. She agreed, and they made the switch. The boys didn't hear this conversation, and I thought it best not to tell them. I did have definite second thoughts, though, about the wisdom of bringing them to this concert.

Nothing happened with my knife-wielding neighbor. As the line moved toward the door, he quietly talked with his girlfriend and minded his own business. My apprehensions began to fade. In fact, I was starting to feel that the concert might not be so bad after all.

"You know, Mr. Meuser," said Bill, "dressed like that, you could pass for someone in his twenties." I was wearing my new jeans, Kevin's Ozzy T-shirt, and the leather jacket.

"Yeah," said Kevin, "you look pretty cool."

"Thanks," I answered. "I do feel about twenty-five again, maybe younger." I was very flattered. I really did feel young. I had a spring in my step, and I think I actually swaggered as I approached the entrance to the arena.

We got to the door. They were taking tickets and checking for weapons. My three students were frisked. I sauntered up to the guard and started to hold up my arms to be searched. He stopped me.

"Just go on in, sir," he said. My heart sank. He had called me "sir" and had not even bothered to frisk me. I guess I wasn't fooling anybody. I undoubtedly looked like a grown-up, and one who wouldn't even own a weapon, much less bring it to a public place. I didn't feel twenty-five anymore. A little of the spring and all of the swagger went out of my step.

We still had plenty of time before the concert. Many seats were available, but the kids wanted to stand in front of the stage. We staked out our claim about twenty feet away. We each took a turn holding our spot while the others bought concert T-shirts, got something to drink, or went to the rest room. I asked Kevin, the most ardent Ozzy fan in our group, to pick out the T-shirt that the class had agreed to buy for me. He carried out this task with relish. Bill and David insisted on helping him select the shirt.

While they were gone, I stood saving our standing room spots. I couldn't help noticing a man in his early twenties standing about fifteen feet away from me in the opposite direction from the stage. He had long hair and clothes that looked as though he had slept in them. Yet it was what he was holding that attracted my attention. In front of him, he clutched a complicated apparatus about fifteen inches tall. Its base was a kind of globe which was made of glass. A couple of other spherical or cylindrical sections were attached to a stem coming out of the globe. A small hose with a mouthpiece on the end came out of the very top. The device was producing smoke, and the man was breathing it in through the hose. His eyes were half closed. He appeared to be in some sort of trance.

As I watched him smoke, I wondered how he had gotten the device past the guards at the entrance. He certainly did

160

not look like a "sir." I turned toward him and gave him a look not unlike one I would give an errant student. Then I looked directly at the smoking apparatus and lowered one eyebrow scornfully.

I didn't expect him to stop what he was doing. I just wanted to register my disapproval, for what that was worth. The reaction I got was totally unexpected. He looked at me, with my eye on the device, hesitated for a moment, and then with both hands raised it in the air in my direction. He was offering me a smoke!

I shook my head and quickly turned around. I was glad that my students weren't there to witness any of that little drama. As luck would have it, however, they were just returning with my new T-shirt and saw the whole thing. It was all they could do not to burst out laughing.

The arena was soon full, and the area in front of the stage was a sea of people. Several times, the four of us had to brace ourselves against the crowd or risk being pushed away from the stage by rowdy late-comers. We managed to maintain our prime location, although I wouldn't have minded too much had we been forced back from the stage just a bit.

The concert finally started with the warm-up band. They were loud but quite forgettable. Sporting the requisite long hair, they sang, danced around the stage, used a fair number of four-letter words, and occasionally waved their guitars in the air or turned and shook their backsides at the audience. This guaranteed their popularity, and the crowd was enthusiastic. They were saving their loudest ovations, however, for the one whom they had really come to see: Ozzy.

The warm-up band finished, and the stage was re-set for the headliner. This seemed to take forever, though no one appeared to mind. When all was ready, an expectant hush fell over the crowd. A smoke machine sent billowing waves of mist onto the stage. Blue lights cast an eerie pall over the entire scene. A recording of the classical piece *Carmina burana* blared over the sound system, emphasizing the mystic, almost medieval atmosphere. As the music rose to a crescendo, the smoke cleared, and a spotlight fixed on a single figure, one resplendent as a knight in shining armor. It was Ozzy.

The crowd went wild. They mostly screamed and cheered but did not applaud. They couldn't. They had only one free hand. With the other they were holding up their flickering butane lighters. In the semi-darkness, the arena looked like a hillside with a thousand burning campfires. Despite the skepticism I had about rock music in general and Ozzy in particular, I had to admit that this man knew how to put on a show. It was pretty impressive.

The lights went up. Ozzy sang. The audience quieted a little, though not much, as they were too excited. What had appeared to be armor on Ozzy was, in fact, leather. The pants were tight-fitting, and the jacket was padded in the chest and thin at the waist. There were even epaulets on the shoulders, which furthered the image of Ozzy as a warrior. He did radiate a certain "machismo." During the third song, he apparently got carried away and excitedly ripped the leather jacket off and tossed it backstage. The crowd roared its approval. He should have kept it on, though. His ample paunch and growing love handles tended to lessen the warrior image he had so carefully cultivated.

All the while, the noise level was truly deafening. My earplugs were my only salvation. I couldn't keep them in continuously or my ears would start to throb. Alternating them in and out kept me from temporarily losing my hearing. My student companions would barely be able to hear anything for about twenty-four hours after the concert.

During the course of the evening, an interesting group of concert-goers attracted our attention. Along the railing of a section of the balcony stood a group of thirty or forty young men. They all had hair at least two feet long, which they draped over the railing. While most people would move and sway with the music, these music lovers remained perfectly motionless except for their heads and hair, which they bobbed up and down in time with the music. They reminded me of chickens pecking for food or of those figures that sit in back windows of cars and have their heads on a spring and wiggle uncontrollably.

Another curious occurrence unfolded right in front of the stage. Suddenly a young man either jumped or was thrown into the air and landed on top of the crowd. Far from being surprised, they kept him airborne, as it were, for about fifteen or twenty seconds. He then disappeared down into the crowd, joining the rest of the throng. This occurred with some regularity, despite efforts of the security guards to prevent it. Once, one of these leapers even passed over me. I was caught a little off guard but managed to help send him on to the people standing next to us. He eventually came to a group that evidently wanted nothing to do with him. They unceremoniously let him fall to the floor. He quickly got up and headed back toward his friends, apparently none the worse for his tumble.

Ozzy sang for about fifty minutes. Then he took a half hour break. After he returned, *with* his leather jacket, he sang for another hour. Though I thought the music well-performed and the rhythm captivating, I had a little trouble catching all of the lyrics. Most of his young audience, on the other hand, knew every song by heart and each time roared their approval on hearing the opening bars. Kevin and Bill turned to me several times to ask me what I thought of songs that were obviously their personal favorites. The noise level prevented me from giving much more than a nod of approval.

The concert ended after several encores. Some people lingered to buy Ozzy paraphernalia, to discuss the music, or simply to drink in the hard rock atmosphere. We left almost immediately. By this time I was anxious to get on the road back to Bridgeport. The boys were, too, because we all had to get up for school in the morning. For a while they discussed the concert and again asked me what I thought of specific songs. Although I was generally complimentary toward the concert, I found it difficult to discuss individual songs. I couldn't resist pointing out, though, that Ozzy's opening theme was a piece of classical music.

The boys soon drifted off to sleep. With little traffic after midnight, we made good time. Even so, it was almost 2:00 AM before my head finally hit the pillow.

The next day, Kevin, Bill, and Dave wore their concert T-shirts. I also wore mine, but over my regular shirt and tie, of

163

course. It seemed that everyone at school had heard about our trip to Dayton to see Ozzy. My third period students, especially, could barely contain their excitement. They wanted to find out every little detail about the concert. A few even stopped by my room before school to ask about it. I told them they would hear all about it during class.

First and second periods flew by. I told them a little about the evening's activities, but I wanted to save most of the story for the class that had sponsored me. It was soon time for third period. Everyone seemed to arrive early, without the usual loitering in the hall or spurious requests to use the rest room before class. They all wanted to hear about the concert.

"How was it?" they all asked even before the bell rang.

"How was what?" I asked. I couldn't resist teasing them just a little.

"Ozzy!" they all said at once.

"Ozzie Nelson?"

"Mr. Meuser!"

"All right," I said, "I'll tell you the whole story."

I related all the details. Kevin, Bill, and David confirmed my story and proudly added their own observations. The class couldn't believe the part where someone actually offered me drugs.

"He didn't freak out," said Kevin. "He just said 'no.'"

"And I hope that's what all of you would do in a similar situation," I added. I knew that some of them would and some would not. At least I expressed my opinion on that issue.

We spent at least half the period discussing the concert. I thanked them for sponsoring me and told them how much I enjoyed it. For their part, they seemed genuinely pleased that I had shown an interest in something that was important to them. I felt a certain kinship with them that had not existed before. Even students at school that I didn't know would, for several days after, come up to me in the hallways and tell me how great it was that I had gone to see Ozzy.

About a month later, in accordance with our wager, Kevin, Bill, David, and their dates accompanied me to a symphony concert. The students were dressed in their best. The hall was elegant, the music was lovely, the audience was absolutely silent during the performance, and the seats were plush and comfortable. No homeless orchestra groupies were hanging around the exits either. Ozzie and Harriet would have been at home here.

It was only then that I realized that I had had something at the Ozzy concert that I wasn't having as much of here: fun.

Danny Boy

I first remember seeing Dan Morgan on a muggy July evening at one of our summer soccer scrimmages. He was one of the few freshmen there. These scrimmages were informal games run by the team captains, and most freshmen tended to stay away because they felt intimidated by the upperclassmen. Not Dan.

Dan reveled at any opportunity to show off his considerable soccer skills to older players and to coaches. He had been somewhat of a star on youth and club soccer teams, always playing in age groups older than his own. He played forward, preferring offense to defense. And though he had superior skills, he played the game like many young stars, totally reliant on his own skills, not willing to make use of the talents of others. I could tell that he would be a good player, but he would need some work.

"Coach Meuser," he tenuously ventured after the scrimmage, "how many freshmen are you going to carry on the varsity team?"

I had been talking to a couple of seniors, and Dan had politely waited for a break in the conversation to ask his question. I knew why he asked it. He wanted to play on the varsity team. I looked down at this thin, curly-haired freshman and saw a little kid. Most of the athletes who had ascended to the varsity squad their freshman year appeared muscular and well-developed and had been shaving since seventh grade. I didn't want to discourage Dan, yet I knew he probably didn't have a chance to beat out any of the many talented juniors and seniors who were returning.

"There is no set number," I said. "To be honest, though, it's pretty unusual for a freshman to make varsity. Jeremy Barker did last year, but he's been the only one for a long time."

"I plan to make it," he declared flatly. At this pronouncement, the seniors still standing there coughed or stifled laughs in the backs of their throats. I ushered Dan away from the group.

"I admire your conviction. I think, maybe, you should set your sights first on doing well on the freshmen team and then moving up to the reserve squad. You have a lot of talent, and I'd rather see you develop it on those teams than sit on the varsity bench. Does that make sense?"

"Yes," he said slowly, "but I'm still going to try to make varsity."

"Well, then, go for it!" I responded. I knew I was going to like this kid.

As it turned out, Dan didn't make the varsity team that year. As I expected, he played on the freshman team for only a few games before moving up to the reserve squad. As the varsity coach, I didn't see him play much. The reserve schedule was different from the varsity, and it was impossible for me to watch more than a couple of their games. I heard of his progress, though, from both the reserve and freshman coaches.

His sophomore year he was again on the reserve squad. I think he felt more than a little disappointed at this. I brought him along on several varsity games, though, and he saw some playing time. He didn't play as much as he would have liked, again, due to the large number of skilled juniors and seniors. Though this wealth of talent made for strong teams, it was

167

frustrating for underclassmen who had to be patient and wait their turn to play varsity.

I also had Dan in one of my second-year algebra classes that year. It gave me a chance to see a different side of Dan. He was a first-rate student, hard-working and studious, but not a bookworm. He was popular with everyone, especially the girls, and he knew it. Gone was the brash, skinny freshman kid from our first meeting. Dan had gained ten to fifteen pounds and had grown three or four inches. He was confident, self-assured, and mature.

I was, therefore, a little surprised one September day to see a small glint of light emanating from Dan's left earlobe as he walked into my classroom. This in itself was not unusual. By this time, plenty of guys were sporting earrings, even at conservative Bridgeport. For male athletes, however, it was a different matter. Earrings were strictly taboo. Each athlete signed a "Code of Conduct" which forbade the use of alcohol or illegal drugs and set standards for proper behavior, both on and off the field. The Code also prescribed grooming regulations, which included a ban on boys' earrings during the athletic season.

I didn't say anything right away. By this point in my career, I preferred to do as much classroom discipline as possible without words, using eye contact instead. In teaching circles, this is known as "the look." I found it to be infinitely more effective than speaking. If a student, for example, were noisily chewing and popping gum, I would stop my lecture, perhaps mid-sentence, slowly turn toward the offender, and look him directly in the eye until I had his undivided attention. Keeping my eyes locked on his, I would raise my index finger and touch my lips, then slowly and silently turn my gaze toward the waste basket in the corner of the room. By the time my eyes had locked back onto the student's, his shoulders would be slumped, and he would reluctantly rise, slink over to the waste basket, and deposit the gum within. Occasionally, a gum popper would protest that it was a fresh piece that I was asking him to relinquish, to which I simply lowered my head and gravely pointed that same index finger toward the waste basket, as though I were the Ghost of Christmas Future showing

Ebenezer Scrooge his own gravestone. By this time, the rest of the class would be chuckling or smiling, and I could hardly resume the lesson without returning them a quick smile of my own. Though we'd had a bit of fun, they all knew that the rules applied to everyone and would be enforced without favoritism. I think most of them felt comfortable and secure in that knowledge.

Accordingly, I began to take attendance, looking around the room to see which seats were vacant. I looked down Dan's row and feigned a double-take as I pretended to get my first look at his earring. My eyes narrowed as I looked at the earring and then into Dan's eyes.

"What?" he asked in two musically descending syllables of protest. I could tell that this one was going to take more than "the look."

"Your earring!" I responded.

"We're not on the soccer field. I can wear it," said Dan, more pleading than defiant.

"Check your Code of Conduct, Dan," I countered. "During soccer season, you're not supposed to wear it at all, not even in the classroom."

"I didn't realize that," he admitted. Dan took his commitments seriously and was bothered by those who didn't. He immediately began to unfasten it from his ear. "At least my dad will be happy I can't wear it. He hates it. He was out-of-town when I got my ear pierced. He nearly killed me when he first saw it."

"I don't blame him," I said. "I'm not that crazy about it myself."

"I'm not that crazy about the school or my dad telling me I can't wear it. But I won't argue."

Others in the class weren't so accommodating. We had a rather heated classroom discussion on the rights of adolescents. Most of the class thought that the Code of Conduct was unfair. How dare anyone tell them how to dress. The students expressing this opinion were largely those not on any athletic team. I let anyone speak who wished but felt a certain obligation to point out that athletic participation was a privilege, not a right, and that being part of a team sometimes meant self-sacrifice. Throughout the discussion, Dan remained virtually silent, preferring to observe the verbal conflagration that he had ignited.

On the field that season, though, Dan was anything but silent. He gravitated toward the thick of the action and scored a couple of amazing goals by jumping well above the crowd and using his head to send the ball to the back of the net. His taste of varsity playing time made him hungry for more. He desperately wanted to prove that he belonged on the varsity team. Still, he remained no better than the juniors and seniors ahead of him. I got him into as many varsity games as I could.

By his junior year, Dan knew he would make varsity. And he did. A starter for many games and the first substitute off the bench in the rest, he worked well with his teammates and seemed to be really coming into his own. About halfway through the season, however, something happened. He stopped playing well. He seemed out of sync with the rest of the team. And most bewilderingly, he lost the intensity that had so characterized his approach to the game. Something was really bothering him, and I needed to find out what it was.

"What's wrong, Dan?" I asked him after practice one day.

"What do you mean?"

"Well, your playing just isn't what it used to be. You're not passing well, and you haven't had a goal or assist in several games now. You're a first-rate soccer player. Yet nothing happens when you're out there on the field. I've got to wonder why."

Not one to run to coaches or teachers at every little hint of trouble, Dan believed in working out his own problems. Yet he evidently had a problem he could not solve himself. He hesitated a little and then spoke quietly.

"They won't play with me."

"What? Who won't play with you?"

"The seniors."

I was dumbstruck. We were midway through a great season. We had been featured in a major article in the sports section of the city's newspaper and became one of the contenders from our area to advance in the state soccer tournament. How a group of kids could jeopardize the team's success by

170

ostracizing a talented teammate was beyond me. I wanted to know who was behind this.

"What seniors?" I asked.

"Just about all of them."

"Why would they do this?"

"I really don't know. It's just so frustrating. I'm getting discouraged. It's like I can't do anything right with them."

"Maybe I should have a talk with them," I suggested.

"No!" said Dan. "That would just make things worse."

"All right. Let me think about the best way to approach this. In the meantime, just keep doing your best. We'll work it out."

I squeezed his shoulder and smiled. He managed a nod and a shrug, and we walked back to the locker room.

I didn't know exactly why the seniors had turned on him, but I could guess. Dan had beaten a senior out of a starting position, then lost it, then gained it back. At first this competition had been a great motivator for both Dan and the senior. Maybe it had turned ugly. The seniors formed a close group, having played together not only through all of high school, but also on their club and recreation teams. If they had closed ranks around one of their own and squeezed out Dan, it would be difficult to reverse that. If it were not that serious, only a squabble, perhaps some encouragement from me could turn things around.

I waited a couple of days so that no one would connect my conversation with Dan to what I would say to the team. We met before practice in our locker room. They were dressed and anxious to get started. We had a game with perennial rival Hampton Heights the next day.

I began the meeting with a few perfunctory announcements and reminders about the upcoming game. I paused before tackling the more difficult topic.

"I was watching our last two game films last night," I began. "I was really troubled by our passing. It just didn't look as sharp as it did at the beginning of the season. I can't figure out what is going on."

I continued with a few examples. "In one series, we had Bob and Dan all alone on the wing. Instead of passing to them, we tried to take the ball straight up the middle. And we got stuffed! That happened again and again. We've got to look for open men and use them, especially on the wings.

"I'll tell you something else. Everyone has to trust each other and be willing to give the ball up to any teammate. If you don't trust even one player with the ball, then it's like we're playing a man down. No team can afford to do that. And certainly not against Hampton Heights.

"I want to scrimmage for most of today's practice. I'm going to choose tomorrow's starting line-up based on what I see in the scrimmage. Now let's get out there and see how well we can pass and how much we trust each other!"

The scrimmage was poetry. The passing was phenomenal, and I told them so. Afterward, Jim Canter, my varsity assistant coach, helped me choose the starting line-up for the big game. Dan was still playing a bit tentatively, even though he received plenty of passes from his teammates. I didn't start him, knowing that he would have lots of playing time tomorrow. Hopefully, he would get his confidence back once he got in the game.

We beat Hampton Heights 3-2. Dan scored one of the goals. He was back on his game, although he continued to battle with the other player for that starting spot, sometimes starting, sometimes being first sub off the bench.

The remainder of the season went pretty well. Through the grapevine, I found out that it hadn't been all the seniors who had snubbed Dan. It was only a few, but they had made their presence known. They may still have felt some resentment over Dan's playing ahead of the senior, but they kept quiet. Dan told me that things were much better. It also helped that we were winning. As most coaches know, winning ball games smoothes over a multitude of ills.

As it turned out, the league title proved elusive. Overconfidence spelled disaster against our last league opponent. We lost a game we should have won handily, and with it, the league championship. We still had the state tournament in which to redeem ourselves, though, and we got a good draw. We sailed through our first tournament game against a considerably weaker team. The second game was with our old rival,

Hampton Heights. To beat them twice in one season would be a real challenge.

On the night of the game, two seniors arrived late to our pre-game meeting. The standard punishment for such tardiness was a seat on the bench. Perhaps a few players on the team thought I would overlook this infraction because of the importance of the game. Most knew that I would do no such thing, including the players who were late.

We arrived at Hampton Heights after a twenty-minute bus ride. I announced the starting eleven just before we warmed up. During warm-ups, Coach Canter privately told me that some of the players were mad that I had benched those two. I pointed out that they should be angry with the two seniors who were late. He agreed.

Despite the rocky start, disgruntled teammates, and the juggling of positions to adjust for the change in personnel, we played well. Neither team scored while my tardy seniors sat on the bench, for which I secretly breathed a sigh of relief. Still, it was a nail-biter. Sometime in the second quarter, Hampton Heights scored. We answered their goal within minutes when Dan stole the ball from a Hampton defender and passed it to Chris Parkes, our leading scorer. Chris sent a shot into the upper right-hand corner of their net to tie the score. Despite our best efforts, though, we just couldn't seem to score again. The game remained tied until the final two minutes when Jeremy Barker, the rock of our defense, fouled a Hampton forward in our penalty area. Hampton Heights scored on the resulting penalty kick and held onto their lead until the clock ran down. In an instant, our season was over.

The ride home was somber. This had been the seniors' last game. I moved through the bus, solemnly shaking their hands and speaking briefly to each one. The last senior I spoke with was Chris Parkes, sitting by himself in the back of the bus. He had scored our only goal of the game and was physically spent. I looked at him and started to shake his hand. He grasped mine, hugged me with his free arm, and began to sob quietly on my shoulder. I let him cry it out.

"It's all right, Chris," I whispered. "Nobody could have given any more than you did tonight. You played a great

173

game. Unfortunately, there aren't any guarantees in athletics. You just do your best, and when the game's over, win or lose, you walk away with your head held high."

Chris nodded. I sat with him for several more minutes, saying nothing. We arrived back at our locker room and unloaded the equipment. The boys went home directly, the coaches after about a half hour of post-game analysis. This was our way of coping with defeat.

Except for its very end, the season had been a great success, though it was hard to realize this in the days that followed our loss to Hampton Heights. We held the banquet about two weeks later. It went very well. We dwelt on the team's successes. Chris Parkes was selected as MVP. I wished him and all the seniors the best of luck for a bright future.

One of our traditions was to announce the next year's team captains at the end of the banquet. The new captains had been elected by secret ballot near the season's finish. No one except the coaches knew who they were. It was, therefore, in an atmosphere of excitement and anticipation that I announced the names of Rob Barrett, junior goalkeeper, and Dan Morgan as our new co-captains. Enthusiastic applause and even cheers from parents and players alike greeted the two choices. I was pleased for both boys, but especially for Dan. He had endured his share of disappointment and frustration during his three years on the team. He was now, finally, on top, in a position of honor and no small authority on the squad. I knew he would be an outstanding leader.

Dan stopped by my room one day after school about the middle of November to talk about plans for next year. He was wearing his earring. The season was over, though, so I didn't say anything. I did glance at it a time or two but did my best *not* to give it "the look." We talked for about an hour. He had several good ideas. He was most passionate, however, about sportsmanship.

"I wish some of our guys had a more professional attitude toward fouling," he said at one point.

"What do you mean?" I asked.

"Well, they take getting fouled so personally. They let a rough foul break their concentration and take them totally out

174

of their game plan. Then they try to retaliate illegally and get caught by the ref, and we lose any momentum we might have had."

"What do you suggest?"

"I don't know. But we've got to convince our guys not to react personally to fouls. If they can dish it out, they had better be able to take it and not go whining to the ref either."

"You're right about that," I concurred. I had been struggling with that problem for years. About the only solution I knew was to bench the offender as an example to the rest of the team. If anyone could come up with a better approach, it would be Dan. Again, I was struck by his maturity and common sense.

I didn't have Dan in class that year, and so saw him only occasionally in the hallways. I wanted to meet with both him and Rob Barrett to plan an indoor soccer party for the team. It was almost Christmas. As there would be plenty of time after the holidays to make those plans, I thought it better to wait until January.

It was four days before Christmas that I got the telephone call. There had been an accident. Dan's car had skidded on a patch of ice near his house. He hadn't been wearing his seat belt and was thrown from the car. He was killed instantly.

I hung up the phone. I felt shock and numbness, but I couldn't cry. I don't know why. Perhaps it was due to the "mantle of leadership." I knew I had much to do, from contacting players and coaches to ordering flowers to offering support to the Morgan family. More likely, it was simply that a protective shell had formed around my emotions from the moment that I heard of Dan's death. I didn't want to face the pain of losing a friend.

Chuck Constantine, the freshmen soccer coach, had known Dan longer than I had. He and I went that evening to pay our respects to Mr. and Mrs. Morgan. Their house was a beehive of activity, with scores of people coming and going. Church, school, and community were all rallying to help them.

Because the school was on its Christmas break, the guidance counselors had organized a special support session for students the next morning. It was held in the school library.

175

Not a seat was empty. Dan's own minister opened the meeting. We soon broke into small groups led by counselors, ministers, or teachers. In my group, the students did most of the talking. I just listened as they shared their memories and thoughts of Dan. After about an hour, Dan's minister closed the meeting with a prayer. Students hugged and cried and didn't seem in any hurry to leave.

I was standing by the door with one of the guidance counselors when a small group of students arrived late. Among them was Chris Parkes. He saw me and immediately walked over. He looked me in the eye, and in that instant I knew that the pain I saw on his face was mirrored in my own. He threw his arms around me, and the protective shell around my emotions shattered. The quiet sobs that followed were not Chris's. The comforted had become the comforter.

I met with the team that evening at Rob Barrett's house. I reminded them that Dan was now in the care of the Almighty. I told them that he would be one of those special people whom no one could ever forget. He would live in all our memories, forever young, strong, and full of life. But I knew that they didn't want memories. They wanted their friend.

I asked Chris Parkes to say a prayer. Players, coaches, and parents hugged. We quietly left Rob's house for the calling hours at the funeral home.

Dan was buried two days later, the day after Christmas.

Though years have passed since then, I think of him often. I don't pretend to understand why his life was cut so short. And though this fine young man profoundly touched the lives of all around him, he never got the chance to lead his team in the sport he loved, never got the chance to attend the college for which he had prepared so long, never got the chance to do just what he wanted when he wanted. Perhaps that was why, at the funeral home, his father had leaned over his son's body and adorned it with the symbol of his youthful independence, something that *he* would have wanted to wear: his earring.

Keri Lynn

She walked in late the first day of class. That in itself was not unusual. On our large campus, a great number of students regularly got lost on opening day. Instead of being apologetic or even slightly embarrassed, though, Keri Lynn lazily and deliberately sauntered to one of two empty desks and tossed her books and purse on top. She was dressed in tight-fitting jeans and a small knit shirt which barely met the top of her jeans. As she sat in the chair, she let out a bored sigh. It was as though she had chosen to be late just to see what would happen. She looked at me through half-closed eyes that appeared to be covered with several pounds of black mascara. I don't think I imagined the slight yet telltale curl in her upper lip. At this moment, I wished that I didn't have to deal with this obnoxious-looking girl. Maybe, I thought, I would get lucky and she would drop the class.

This was the first of many times that year when I would question my own sanity and judgment. For quite some time, I had been teaching the advanced math classes at Bridgeport. The students in those classes were middle to upper-middle class, and college-bound. They rarely caused trouble and were

177

highly motivated. I had it made! Why I *volunteered* to pilot a new introductory algebra program, I'll never know. Maybe I was intrigued by the new program's claims of success, especially with lower-level math students. Maybe I was bored with my cushy assignment. Maybe I was just plain nuts!

Whatever the reason, I now stood before a varied group of kids, most of whom had no intention of darkening the doorway of any institution of higher learning. To be fair, some of them were just a year behind their college-prep friends. They were not strong in math but would work diligently and progress through the math curriculum at a slower pace. They might attend college or at least a two-year technical school. These, I felt, were the ones I was really here for, not for kids who wouldn't try, and certainly not for someone like Keri Lynn.

On this first day, I tried to deflect her apparent hostility. "I know that some of you may have had difficulty in finding your way around on the first day," I said to the whole class. "We'll start keeping track of tardiness tomorrow."

"Oh, I know my way around," she bragged. "I just had to pee."

I must admit that I was taken aback by her crude choice of words as well as her attitude, especially on the first day of class. Most students wait at least a couple of days to see how far they can push a teacher. If this, though, were her first salvo, I was prepared to return it in kind.

"First of all," I said sternly, "we don't use language like that in this classroom." I lowered my head, looked at her over the tops of my glasses, and added, "Secondly, if that's your way of *requesting* a detention, we can certainly arrange it for you." I made liberal use of the "royal we." It was so effective, so coolly distancing.

It was Keri Lynn's turn to be taken aback, though she quickly recovered. "I don't want no detention!"

"Then make sure you're on time tomorrow," I said with finality. Keri Lynn didn't speak. She frowned. As I proceeded with the opening day formalities, I smugly congratulated myself on my well-practiced disciplinary skills. I would need to be watchful and nip any problems with this girl in the bud.

178

The pilot math program began successfully enough. It required less lecture and more individual student work than a traditional class. I could spend most of my time circulating around the room helping students who needed it. Most students responded pretty well to the new format. Keri Lynn did not.

Though she did make it to class on time after the first day, she appeared to have an unquenchable desire to draw attention to herself in a wide variety of ways. Not self-motivated, she required continual prodding to stay on task. If she had a question about her class work, which was often, she behaved like a spoiled child, expecting my help instantly. Never mind that others in the class had raised their hands ahead of her. She needed help, and she wanted it now. Of course, I always made her wait her turn. During this time she would show her displeasure by exhaling loudly, by noisily rummaging through her purse for who knows what, or even by announcing to the class that the assignment was impossible. Here sat a girl, I thought, who craved attention.

Keri Lynn failed the first quarter. She had almost no math skills. She felt frustrated but seemed unable to do anything about it. Perhaps if she had done even a little homework, she might have had a better chance. She did virtually none, however. I had sent a progress report home midway through the grading period but received no response from her parents. When I informed her of the first-quarter grade, I asked her about her dismal homework record.

"I don't have no time for homework," she replied.

Every fiber of my being wanted to correct her grammar. Normally I would have done so without even thinking. Something about her tone, though, told me that she had temporarily lowered her tough-girl facade. Her voice had none of its usual hostility. It conveyed sincerity and was almost pleading. I ignored her grammar.

"Why not?" I asked. My own tone registered concern rather than censure.

"Well, after school I go to work till 6:30. After that I pick up my little sister from the sitter's. Then I have to clean the house and get dinner ready. Once I get my sister bathed and put to bed, I usually fall asleep."

"Where are your mom and dad?" I asked.

"Oh, they're divorced. I live with my mom. But she works a lot of hours, and I have to help out. I have to take care of Shauna. She's my little sister." At this last mention of her sister, her eyes twinkled. She obviously loved her sister. Keri Lynn suddenly seemed less like a spoiled child and more like a young mother.

"Isn't there anyone who can help you?" I asked, still shocked by her seemingly unmanageable situation.

"Not really. My grandma helps sometimes, but she's got to work, too." She paused then added, "There is Eddie. He's my mom's boyfriend, but he's the biggest waste. He just comes over and eats our food and tries to tell me what to do."

The bell for lunch had rung a few minutes before, but Keri Lynn had stayed to tell her story. I asked when she got to school in the morning. She told me that she usually arrived just before the tardy bell. I suggested that she come a little early to my room and use that time for homework. She looked doubtful but promised to try.

She took me by surprise the next morning by actually showing up for her homework session. We worked for about fifteen minutes. She seemed to understand everything we did. As she left for her own first-period class, she did something that I had never seen her do before. She smiled.

In the weeks that followed, Keri Lynn made it to my classroom before school two or three mornings a week. She not only raised her grade to a respectable "C," but also began to show a different side of her character in class. She always greeted me with a smile. I even started to correct her spoken grammar. She would give me benignly exasperated looks, as though I were some old fuss-budget whom she was obliged to humor. Perhaps I was exactly that. Nevertheless, her grammar did improve.

Gradually I noticed a change in Keri Lynn that was more than a mere improvement in grammar or courtesy. This change was profound. She transformed from a card-carrying member of the "High School Troublemakers Association" to one of the large majority of responsible students. Even her appearance improved. She wore more tasteful clothing, and her eyes also no longer looked like they were being attacked by tarantulas. It was as though she had changed the way she viewed herself. Though I didn't know what had caused this transformation, I hoped that her success in math class was at least reinforcing it.

The school year progressed quickly, and our Indian-summer autumn gave way to colder weather. Light jackets were replaced with winter coats. I had bundled up one morning and was walking between periods from my tutoring assignment in the cafeteria study hall to my classroom in the math building. As I rounded the corner by one bank of lockers, I noticed a boy walking slowly in my direction. With his eyes seemingly closed and his head rhythmically bobbing up and down, he marched to the beat of an invisible drummer, one whose music he heard through the earphones clamped to his head. A cord wound its way from the headset to the pocket of his large winter coat. Because any radios or tape players were strictly forbidden at school, I stopped him.

"You're not allowed to have headsets at school," I said.

"Huh?"

"That headset!" I repeated. "You may not have them on school property. You'll have to turn it into the office."

"I'm not givin' up my headset. No way!" he blustered.

"You're welcome to talk to an administrator and plead your case," I offered.

"No way!" came his less than creative reply.

"Then you'll have to give it to me," I concluded. "I'll put your name on it, and you can pick it up later."

"No way!"

At this point, he abruptly decided that he wasn't going to win this verbal argument, especially with a two-word vocabulary. Accordingly, he took matters into his own hands, or rather his own feet. He ran.

In the "old days," my colleagues and I would have chased down such a student. Once, when faced with two ne'er-do-wells who had run out of the cafeteria at lunch, left school property, and split up, I chose to go after the slower-looking

181

one. I soon caught up with him and brought him back to the office, where he quickly informed on his partner in crime. An assistant principal nabbed the second kid in his first class after lunch.

Times were now different. In the current litigious atmosphere, we were told not to touch students, let alone bring them to the office by the collar. Perhaps our nineteenth-century disciplinary tactics were out of place in the twentieth century, but we were left with few options when dealing with recalcitrant students who refused to return to the office.

As I watched the student speed away, I looked around for someone who might be able to identify him. Seeing no one, I returned to my room feeling extremely frustrated. My fifth-period class worked very well and soon restored my good humor, although the rule-breaker's escape still gnawed at me a little.

After class, Keri Lynn took quite some time to pack up her book bag before she left. By the time she was ready to leave, she was the only one left in the room.

"How's everything with you, Keri Lynn," I asked, just making conversation.

"Fine," she answered slowly. She paused, and I realized that she wanted to talk to me.

"What is it, Keri Lynn?"

"I know who it was," she said quietly, glancing around the empty room to make sure we were alone.

"Who what was?" I asked, not comprehending.

"I know the kid with the headset who ran away from you," she explained. "I was just around the corner at my locker and saw the whole thing. I made sure you didn't see me, though. I couldn't tell you anything if I thought anyone might find out. That's why I waited till now to tell you."

She told me the student's name. I assured her that her name would remain a secret and thanked her for her help. I told her how proud I was of her. Though I was glad that student with the headset would be brought to justice, I was much more gratified that Keri Lynn had trusted me enough to tell me who he was.

She had a question for me before she left for lunch.

"Why are you so strict about students following the rules?"

"Because the rules have to apply to everyone," I responded. "What would happen if I started *choosing* the students whom I would discipline? What if I started playing favorites?"

"Nobody would respect you, that's for sure."

"Exactly," I said. "The only *choosing* involved is the student's choice to misbehave. It's that choice that I must deal with."

"What about adults?" she asked. "What happens when they mess up?"

"Well, I guess they have to suffer the consequences, too."

She started to say something, then evidently changed her mind.

"I've got to go," she said quickly.

"Bye, and thanks again for your help."

I wondered what was bothering her. Because I didn't want to intrude into her life, I would just have to wait until she decided she could confide in me

Christmas soon came upon us. On the last day before the break, Keri Lynn gave me a lovely card. In it, she thanked me for the extra help I had given her and mentioned that she was thinking about attending the local community college after graduation in the spring. She wished me a happy holiday. It was, sadly, the last time I would associate the word *happy* with Keri Lynn.

Things started to go wrong after the first of the year. It started with one or two absences from school. When she returned, I asked her if everything was all right. Her silent nod was less than convincing. The absences soon became more frequent. Though her first few were listed as "excused," they quickly turned into "unexcused." Finally, "truant" was listed beside her name on the attendance sheets. Because all phone calls home went unanswered, I turned to her guidance counselor, Barbara Kohl.

"What's going on with Keri Lynn Meadows?" I asked. "She was doing so well, and now she's listed as truant."

Barb picked up Keri Lynn's student record folder, which was already lying on top of the pile on her desk. She glanced through it, shaking her head. Finally she looked up at me.

183

"I'm sure you know that Keri Lynn has a lot of problems," she began.

"Not really," I had to admit. "I know her home situation isn't the best, but she seemed to be coping." I had never been one to do too much browsing through student records, having neither the time nor the inclination. I preferred to start each year with a clean slate, forming my own opinion of students as I got to know them.

"Well, she has," continued Barb. "Children Services has suspected child abuse over the years but could never establish it. Some of it may have been sexual, but they don't know that for sure either. They suspect her mother's boyfriend but haven't filed any charges. In any event, Keri Lynn has run away."

I couldn't believe it. She had seemed so happy before Christmas. She was starting to put it all together. I couldn't believe she had just left. I had to wonder about her sister, too.

"What about Shauna?" I asked. "Keri Lynn would never leave her sister in those circumstances."

"I guess Keri Lynn took Shauna to her grandmother's. They're letting her keep the little girl until the situation is resolved."

"Is there anything we can do?" I asked.

"Not really," answered Barb. "If she happens to come to your class, let me know immediately."

"OK," I said. I left Barb's office in a daze. Of course I felt sorry for Keri Lynn's miserable situation. But also, rather selfishly, I felt hurt that she hadn't trusted me enough to ask for my help—not that I could have done anything. Perhaps I could have steered her toward someone who would.

I recalled our conversation when she helped me nab the "headsetter." I knew she had wanted to tell me something else. Whether or not she would have told me all her troubles, I don't know. I feel certain, though, that she would have answered her own question about what happens when adults misbehave a little differently than I did that day. She would have said, *When adults break the rules, the kids pay the price.*

Keri Lynn never came back to class. She had gone to her dad's, who lived about an hour from Bridgeport. He was eventually awarded custody of both Keri Lynn and her sister. Keri Lynn, who had recently turned eighteen, dropped out of school to work and to take care of her sister. She evidently had plans to get her G.E.D., a high school equivalency diploma.

She stopped by school once and spoke with Barb Kohl. Barb said that she was concerned about what her teachers thought of her but didn't want to see any of them. I wanted to be able to tell her that I thought very highly of her and that I wished her the best in earning her G.E.D. I never saw her again, however, so I never got that chance. I don't know if she ever obtained her diploma or if her life improved at her dad's. I could only hope.

Thinking back to her first day in my class, I cringed as I remembered my wish that she drop out. That would be the last thing I would wish for now. I recalled a comment made to me years earlier by an experienced elementary teacher: "If you want to teach, you've got to be willing to hug the little kid who smells." I suddenly understood the full import of her remark. I had to ask myself whether I had joined the profession to teach the student who wanted my help but didn't really need it, or to try to reach the kid who desperately needed help but didn't want it. After no small struggle with this enigma, I realized the obvious answer: both, and everyone in between.

The Santa Candle

Allison Barnes sat in the back of the room and rarely opened her mouth. She was the kind of student who might easily go unnoticed. She wore no make-up, preferred baggy pants and old sweatshirts, and had succumbed to the popular teen fashion of shaving her hair on a selected portion of her head. Most students who did that looked positively grotesque. Allison, however, had shaved a section of hair on the back of her head at the base of her neck. It was possible for her, if she so chose, to camouflage that rebelliously close-cropped section by merely combing her long hair over it. She was definitely a free spirit.

As I was to find out later, she considered me to be compulsively neat and controlling. This was, no doubt, a fairly accurate assessment. At any rate, she didn't feel that she would thrive in a room where she had to raise her hand before she spoke or push in her chair after she left her seat. To make matters worse, she hated math. She had done well in arithmetic but had fallen by the mathematical wayside when she ventured into the abstract realms of algebra and geometry.

The class in which she was enrolled was Algebra II. I started on the first day as I had for many years prior to that.

"Good morning," I began. "My name is Mr. Meuser. Welcome to Algebra II. As I call your name, please take your seat. If I mispronounce your name, be sure to let me know." I then went over a few class rules and procedures and told them a little about myself, my wife, and my daughter.

Having completed these introductory formalities, we plunged into a review of Algebra I. I tried to show them the reasoning behind some of the procedures that many of them might have learned by rote. We explored those concepts in a less abstract way, with numbers instead of algebraic letters. I passed out a sheet of review problems for homework, which I asked them to begin during the last ten minutes of the period. I circulated around the room, answering questions and offering advice. Most of the kids seemed to be excited about learning new twists on old topics. All in all, I thought, a great opening class.

Allison was not impressed. She was more than a little irritated at having to work on mathematics the first day. In her view, the first day's activities should have been restricted to introductions, perhaps a presentation of classroom rules, and most certainly a chance to chat with friends about events of the bygone summer vacation. The fact that I gave homework on the first day was totally "un-cool."

The review material that I presented was to Allison brand new. She didn't understand my explanations any more than she had understood those of past math teachers. Because I was reviewing, I felt comfortable in proceeding at a faster pace than I would have with new material. For Allison, this pace was frenetic. She was overwhelmed.

The situation continued like this for her until about the third week of school. We were graphing positive and negative numbers on a number line. Several students were having trouble distinguishing negative numbers from the operation of subtraction because both use a minus sign. After making several attempts at explaining it, I realized that I was getting nowhere with them. I walked from in front of the blackboard to the cupboard in the back of the room. I strode with great purpose, which belied the fact that I didn't know what I was going to do. I was desperately grasping for an idea as well as a physical model as I rummaged through the boxes in the cupboard.

Then I saw it. There on a shelf sat the only Christmas decoration that I had in the room: a large, squat candle made in the image of Santa Claus. I think it had been a gift to my wife from one of the members of her children's choir at church. It was a silly-looking Santa, not meant to be realistic. Actually, it looked like Santa had been to the Christmas punch bowl once too often. I had brought it to school the previous Christmas so that I would have at least some bit of decoration to display.

I took Santa and held him up to the number line I had drawn on the board. His nose was facing right.

"Addition," I said, "is when Santa is going forward." I moved Santa along the number line several spaces to the right. He bobbed happily up and down as he moved along the line.

"Subtraction," I continued, "is when Santa is going backwards." As I moved Santa to the left, I let out a small, high-pitched, but urgent cry, as though Santa were being forced backwards against his will. Several students chuckled.

"Positive and negative numbers are simply locations on the number line. Whether those locations are positive or negative depends on whether they are to the right or left of zero. In other words, if Santa moves backwards from zero three spaces, he ends up at the location on the number line called 'negative three.'" I let out a little cry again as I moved Santa to the left three spaces from zero and landed on -3.

We did several examples with Santa to illustrate adding and subtracting positive and negative numbers. Pretty basic stuff. Most of those who had been having difficulty were nodding their understanding. Those who had already understood it were either chuckling at the silliness of my example or rolling their eyes heavenward in exasperation. For Allison, though, it was a revelation. That Santa Candle had lit a flame where before there had been only darkness.

I noticed a definite change in her attitude and performance from that day on. She started to get A's on the tests. She put problems on the board and raised thoughtful questions in class. I assumed that, for her, mathematics had finally clicked. I didn't find out until the following year what had happened. For a senior English class assignment, she wrote an essay about her experiences in my math class. She related the incident with the Santa Candle. She said that once that "light bulb" was turned on, she understood everything that I said in class. Instead of dreading math class, she looked forward to it. She gave me all the credit and finished the essay with numerous compliments on my teaching style. With Allison's permission, her English teacher had shown it to me. Of course, I was extremely flattered. This was the kind of testimonial that a high school teacher receives maybe once a career.

I basked in the glow of her essay for quite some time afterward. I told other teachers about the effectiveness of the Santa Candle and even had requests from some of them to borrow it. They reported that it worked beautifully. "Santa" became a regular performer in my classroom. He actually gained some small notoriety around school. Amid all of this educational bonhomie, however, disaster struck.

I had used Santa to illustrate a point in my fourth period calculus class. I made the mistake of tooting my own metaphorical horn a little too loudly, pointing out what a wonderful visual aid it had been to so many students. This evidently was just too much for a group of them. I had placed Santa on a stand in the front of the room. After the class was over, I went to the stand to get the candle and put it away. It was gone.

The next day I received an unsigned communiqué in my school mailbox. On it was a Xeroxed picture of Santa next to a handgun with the words "Search for Santa" at the top of the page. Attached was a ransom note. It was written on a computer but made to look like the letters were cut out of a magazine. The note demanded "A's" for all fourth period calculus students in exchange for Santa's safe return. At least I knew that the kidnapper still had Santa and that he was probably all right.

No one in fourth period would admit to taking him. Several students in class said they would reveal the identity of the kidnapper in exchange for extra-credit points. Although tempted, I resisted these offers. This would set a bad precedent. I was not going to negotiate with terrorists or their compatriots.

On day three of the crisis, another teacher's study group used my classroom during lunch, so the room was open for a time while I was in the cafeteria. When I returned from lunch, I noticed something unusual on my normally tidy desk. At first, I thought it might be a piece of scrap paper. Upon closer examination, I realized that it was a lump of burned candle wax. A note beside it claimed, "This used to be Santa's ear. If you want the rest of him, you must agree to give all your fourth-period students 'A's.'" Someone was going to an awful lot of trouble to make me think Santa had been harmed.

Days passed. During this time, I was obviously unable to use Santa as a visual aid. I tried using a small bottle of correction fluid dubbed "R2-D2" from the movie *Star Wars* in its place. That didn't work very well. He didn't have a nose, so no one could tell what direction he was pointing.

I tried to make fourth period feel guilty. I threatened them. I pleaded with them. I begged. All to no avail. I told all my other classes about the kidnapping and encouraged them to keep their eyes and ears open. The "Search for Santa" took on a greater magnitude and urgency.

To make matters worse, I couldn't even use Santa as a Christmas decoration. The kidnapping had taken place about two weeks before Christmas. With Santa gone, I just didn't have the enthusiasm to bring in another decoration.

Then, on the day before Christmas break, I received a beautifully wrapped present from a group of students in fourth period. The present came in a large, department store shirt box which had a definite bulge in its middle. I knew what had to be inside. I tore open the wrapping and opened the box. Yes, there was Santa lying in the middle of the box, unharmed. Other items lay in the box, as well, including a book of crossword puzzles, which they knew I liked to do every day, a tube of hand cream for my chalk-chapped hands, and a Christmas book for my daughter. The final gift in the box was a grooming kit containing a comb, nail clippers, and a file. I'm not exactly sure why they gave me that. Perhaps it was a hint that I wasn't as obsessively tidy as Allison Barnes had thought.

Because Santa was returned, all was forgiven. I thanked them for the gifts. I was touched by their thoughtfulness. Moreover, I marveled at the amount of effort they had put into the entire kidnapping plot. Of course the entire class was in on it. To celebrate his safe return, everyone had brought in Christmas cookies and refreshments. Needless to say, we took an unscheduled break from calculus that day.

Now that he was back, Santa could resume his role in helping students visualize positive and negative numbers. The search for Santa was over. The search for each student's candle to light the darkness could continue.

I didn't realize it immediately, but my own search had come to a milestone. I had been to the mountain. Allison Barnes had seen me there and had joined me on the journey. Her essay affected me deeply, not because I felt flattered, but because I felt humbled. If the Santa Candle had lit her path toward understanding, it had lit mine too. I saw not only the path to the mountain, but also a whole gathering of students who were on that path.

Even those students who kidnapped Santa had been with me to the mountain. I realized that they gave me much more than the crossword puzzles or hand lotion in the beautifully wrapped Christmas box. They gave me their love.

Birdie Langley, in her speech at my first-ever teacher conference long ago, had been right. Touching the hearts of students is incredibly rewarding. But being touched by *them* is the gift of a lifetime.

191